HEAD START I

English for Cross-cultural Communication

Patricia Che

關於作者

車蓓群

1985 到 2007 年間，身為大學老師的我，藉著各種校內外的課程，有幸接觸到不同程度與不同需求的學習者。在他們身上，我反覆的看到二個現象：第一是無論他們的程度與需求為何，大部分的學習者，都將英語視為一門深奧嚴肅需要努力研讀與分析的學科，而忘了語言本身存在的目的並不是為了要供人們研讀，而是為了要溝通；也就是說，語言的使用除了有嚴肅的課題外，更有趣味與生活的面向。第二則是語言的學習，常獨立於語言所相互依存的社會文化習俗，及溝通所使用的身體語言之外。

這二個現象讓我很想做一本教科書，是不那麼嚴肅、帶點小趣味，可以直接利用在生活中、但卻直接切中現今社會中十分重要的種種跨文化議題。34 年英語學習與 22 年英語教學的經驗告訴我，即使沒有正經八百、或正襟危坐的研讀英語，學習者還是可以開開心心，並且信心十足的使用這個語言來溝通。After all, I did it. I hope you can be just like me: enjoy English and allow it to be part of your daily life!

給讀者

國際化、國際化公民、地球村等等，都是這些年喊的震天價響的一些口號，帽子很大，理想很高，但到底要如何落實呢？當然，學英文是諸多方法中的一個，也可以是很有效的一個，可是只要會看 News week、聽 CNN 就表示英文可以溝通了嗎？

那可是大錯特錯。溝通，而且是有效率不會產生誤解的溝通，其實除了包含聽說讀寫四種技能之外，還有身體語言、對周遭環境的認識與理解，另外更重要的是對這個語言的文化有所認知。在英文逐漸成為國際通用語的同時，我們不但有美式英文、英式英文、紐澳英文、更有印度英文以及新加坡英文等；如果在學英文的過程中，我們只知美國文化，這是很可悲且值得警惕的事。

本書就是依照這樣的理念，將跨文化溝通與身體語言的學習，藉由自美國來台灣生活的一家人帶出，架構在聽說讀寫的基本技巧上，利用吃、喝、玩、樂工作及生活的各種場景，來反覆練習有效溝通時所需的種種語言及非語言的知識與技能。

因此，本書中每一個單元都以生活中某一個面向為主題，以聽、說、讀、寫的方式進行內容的介紹。每一個主題常使用的關鍵字會先以圖片來介紹，接著將這些圖片中的字詞或短句放在對話中，再將這些詞彙運用在接下來的聽力練習裡。反覆之後，我們利用引導式口語練習，將前面介紹的詞彙直接放進不同場景的對話中，去嘗試真正使用它們。接著我們將與主題相關的跨文化溝通知識以短文方式呈現，並佐以閱讀測驗練習。下一個單元則是有系統的介紹在段落短文寫作中，學習者最常碰到的一些問題；以 1、3、5、7 課次介紹新的主題，2、4、6、8 課次複習的方式來進行。另外，依據大量閱讀的重要性及跨文化議題的多面向，我們還在每個單元中安排了兩篇深度閱讀來分享更多知識。同時，為了讓學習的成效更為明顯，我們還針對每個單元製作四張學習單，讓讀者可以隨時挑戰自己對這個主題的理解。

我們衷心希望能以這些生活化的主題和反覆練習的架構，讓所有讀者能在英文進步的同時，對跨文化溝通有多一層的了解，進而成為真正的國際化公民。

車蓓群謹識

Contents

Content Chart

Unit	Where It All Begins	Listening and Oral
1	I'm Christopher Parker. Please call me Chris.	Greetings
		Introductions
2	Turn right at the corner.	Asking for and Giving Directions
		Making Telephone Calls
3	The meeting is scheduled for Friday.	Making Appointments
		Expressing Preferences for Objects, Activities, Etc.
4	I can't stand it anymore!	Complaining About Personal Proximity
		Complaining About Personal Questions
5	How would you like your bread?	Ordering Food
		Complaining About Food
6	I'd like to ask that tall, slender girl out.	Describing Physical Appearance
		Extending and Rejecting Invitations
7	The total is NT$500.	Making Purchases
		Returning or Exchanging Merchandise
8	Sales Manager Wanted	Describing Personality Traits
		Expressing Preferences for People

Short Reading	Writing	Advanced Readings
What's in a Name?	Topic Sentences/Choose a Topic Sentence	Business Etiquette for Addressing Others
	Subject-Verb Agreement: Indefinite Pronouns	Working with Foreign Cultures
Traffic on Venus and Mars	Review: Topic Sentences/Choose a Topic Sentence	Talking Without Walking on Thin Ice
	Review: Subject-Verb Agreement: Indefinite Pronouns	Equality in the Workplace: Much Needs to Be Done
From "Time" to "Time"	General or Specific	The Secretary Is on Guard
	Use Parallelism Correctly	My Time or Your Time?
Beyond Words	Review: General or Specific	Listen for Real
	Review: Use Parallelism Correctly	An Eye for an Eye
All About the Taste?	Avoid Irrelevance	Bugs for Breakfast
	Avoid Shifts in Person	What Not to Eat in India
Happy Meal or Rumbling Stomach?	Review: Avoid Irrelevance	International Dining—Do Your Research!
	Review: Avoid Shifts in Person	Knives, Forks, and Chopsticks
A Gift from the Heart	Supporting Sentences	Holy Cow! A Leather Jacket!
	Avoid Shifts in Tense	Environmental Ideas for Gift Giving
How to Flunk an Interview	Review: Supporting Sentences	To Veil or Not to Veil?
	Review: Avoid Shifts in Tense	You Are What You Wear

Acknowledgements

All articles in this publication are adapted from the works by:

Amelia Smolar, Betty Carlson, Gail Sharpe, Jamie Blackler, Jason Grenier, Jeff Zeter (Group), Joe Chan, Karl Nilsson, Katherine S. Leppert, M. J. McAteer, Matthew Wilson, Michelle Waitzman, Ming Wong, Miranda Marquit, Paul Geraghty, Suzanne E. Carter, Suzanne Elvidge, and Toni Jordan.

Photo Credits

All pictures in this publication are authorized for use by:

David S. Maehr, Dreamstime, iStockphoto, and ShutterStock.

Meet the Parkers

The Parkers have just moved from the U.S. to Taiwan.

Henry Parker (father of the family): He is a freelance writer.

Chris Parker (Henry and Laura's son): He is on an exchange program to study Chinese in Taiwan's university.

Laura Parker (mother of the family): She is about to start working as a CEO in Taiwan.

I'm Christopher Parker. Please call me Chris.

🎧 Greetings

Tips for You

1. Couldn't be better! 好得很！
2. Can't complain! 一切都還順心！

3. work on 致力於…，為…費心
4. project [`pradʒɛkt] *n*. 企畫，計畫

Listening Practice

Listen to the greetings, and choose the best response to each of them.

_____ 1. (A) Very well, thank you.
(B) No, that's not mine.
(C) I'm Patty. And you?
(D) Yes, I am fine.

_____ 5. (A) I haven't seen anything yet.
(B) Yes, I got up early today.
(C) I've been busy with work.
(D) No, I didn't stay up last night.

_____ 2. (A) I am a sales manager.
(B) Yes, I am a high school
teacher.
(C) I am looking for a shoe store.
(D) How do you do, Ms. Wang?

_____ 6. (A) Can you tell me about it?
(B) Yes, I have everything now.
(C) Can't complain.
(D) No, I don't have anything with
me.

_____ 3. (A) I am going to the library.
(B) Couldn't be better.
(C) It is going there.
(D) Can't you go with us?

_____ 4. (A) Nice to meet you, too.
(B) Yes, you are very nice.
(C) Sorry to hear that.
(D) No, I haven't seen that.

 Introductions

❶

Let me ¹***introduce*** *myself. My name is Eric Wang.*

❹

Hi, my name is Alexander Lin. You can call me Alex.

❷

Hi, I'm Joy—Joy Chen. I live next door. What's your name?

❺

*I'd like to introduce myself. I'r Catherine Fang. I ²**majored i** ³**business administration** in college.*

❸

Hey, I'd like you to meet my best friend, Cory.

❻

*Have you met Eddie yet? He's my ⁴**roommate**.*

Tips for You

1. introduce [ˌɪntrəˈdjus] *v.* 介紹
2. major [ˈmedʒɚ] *v.* 主修
   major [ˈmedʒɚ] *n.* 主修…的學生；主修科目

3. business administration 企業管理
4. roommate [ˈrumˌmet] *n.* 室友

Work in groups of two or three and complete each of the dialogues. Use the expressions on the previous page wherever appropriate.

1

A: _____

_____

B: Hi, I'm _____.

A: Glad to be your new neighbor. Do you need any help?

B: Thanks for asking. I think everything is fine here.

2

A: Hi, _____. Nice to see you here.

B: Yeah, what a surprise!

A: _____

_____

B: Oh, hi, Sally. Nice to meet you.

3

A: _____

_____

B: Nice to meet you, _____ (name of your partner). My name is _____.

A: Nice to meet you, too. It's a nice party, isn't it?

B: Yeah, it is. I'm having a great time.

4

A: Hi, boss, you ¹**work out** here, too?

B: That's right! I've been working out in this ²**gym** for a year.

A: So, it looks like we work AND work out in the same places. Oh, _____

_____.

B: Oh, hi, _____. It's a pleasure to meet you. Your wife/husband is one of the best workers I've ever had.

Tips for You

1. work out   運動

2. gym [dʒɪm] *n.* 健身房

Short Reading

What's in a Name?

Mr. Huck Morris, a 28-year-old American ¹**CEO**, had just met Mr. Hideto Tanaka for the first time. Mr. Tanaka, a 60-year-old Japanese CEO, had just ²**flown in** from Tokyo to New York. Mr. Morris was very ³**eager** to close a ⁴**promising** ⁵**deal** with Mr. Tanaka. When Morris greeted Mr. Tanaka in his office, he said, "Nice to meet you, Hideto." All of a sudden, Mr. Tanaka looked offended and uncomfortable. At the end of the day, Mr. Morris failed to close the deal. "What went wrong?" he ⁶**couldn't help but** ask himself.

Like everyone in business, Mr. Morris only got one chance to make a first ⁷**impression**, and he failed—terribly. His poor understanding of Japanese culture caused him to make a mistake—calling Mr. Tanaka by his ⁸**first name**—that cost him a business deal. If Mr. Morris had done his homework before the meeting, he would have known that to the Japanese, only close friends and family members are allowed to use a person's first name. The use of last name is a must for strangers in business associates. Besides, it is unthinkable to ⁹**address** an elder person by his or her first name. To this young CEO, no homework done means a ¹⁰**disappointment** and loss

Despite such a terrible beginning, Mr. Morris's story has a happy ending. Later, Mr. Morris decided to call Mr. Tanaka, ¹¹**apologize** to him, and ask for another meeting. He made sure to address and ¹²**interact** with Mr. Tanaka in a way that is respectful and proper in Japanese culture. It was a valuable lesson to Mr. Morris: always "do your homework" before meeting with someone from a different culture.

Tips for You

1. CEO (= Chief Executive Officer) 執行長
2. fly in   飛抵
3. eager [`igɚ] *adj.* 急切的
4. promising [`prɑmɪsɪŋ] *adj.* 有希望的
5. deal [dil] *n.* 交易
6. cannot help but V   不禁⋯
7. impression [ɪm`prɛʃən] *n.* 印象
8. first/last name *n.* 名 / 姓

9. address [ə`drɛs] *v.* 稱呼；*n.* 稱謂
10. disappointment [ˌdɪsə`pɔɪntmənt] *n.* 失望
    disappointed [ˌdɪsə`pɔɪntɪd] *adj.* 失望的
    disappointing [ˌdɪsə`pɔɪntɪŋ] *adj.* 令人失望的
11. apologize [ə`pɑlədʒaɪz] *v.* 道歉
    apology [ə`pɑlədʒɪ] *n.* 道歉
12. interact [ˌɪntɚ`ækt] *v.* 互動
    interaction [ˌɪntɚ`æktʃən] *n.* 互動

Reading Comprehension

I. *Based on the reading, mark each of the following statements about Mr. Morris with T (True) or F (False).*

_____ 1. He is thirty-two years younger than Mr. Tanaka.

_____ 2. He had done his homework about Japanese culture before the first meeting.

_____ 3. He successfully closed a promising deal the first time he met Mr. Tanaka.

_____ 4. He should have called Mr. Tanaka by his last name when they first met.

_____ 5. He has worked for Mr. Tanaka for many years.

II. *Based on the reading, choose the correct answer to each of the following questions.*

( ) 1. The reading is mainly about _____.

(A) how to close business deals

(B) how to properly address a person from Japan

(C) how to speak Japanese

(D) how to get along with an old businessman

( ) 2. Mr. Tanaka felt offended and uncomfortable because _____.

(A) Mr. Morris called him by his first name

(B) he had to fly from Tokyo to New York for the meeting

(C) Mr. Morris didn't apologize for being late for the meeting

(D) there was not enough time for him and Mr. Morris to close the deal

( ) 3. To the Japanese, only _____ are allowed to address a person by his or her first name.

(A) co-workers   (B) strangers

(C) teachers   (D) close friends

Writing I

Topic Sentences/Choose a Topic Sentence

主題句 (topic sentence) 也就是每個段落的中心思想。因此，主題句具有提綱挈領的作用，也是全文內容的主軸。一旦決定了主題句，作者便可有效、清楚地判斷，哪些內容適合納入段落中，並轉化成句子。

Exercise: 選出最適合當作以下每個段落的主題句。

( ) 1. _____

The Thai usually greet each other with a nod and a prayer-like gesture called "wai." To the Japanese, a bow is the most common greeting, especially in a traditional setting. The Europeans and the North Americans usually shake hands to greet each other.

(A) The meaning of a gesture is different from culture to culture.

(B) Every culture has its own common greeting.

(C) Asian cultures are different from one another.

(D) There are many cultures in the world.

( ) 2. _____

When a person from Greece, Turkey, or southern India shakes his or her head, it means he or she "understands" you or "agrees" with you. However, if this gesture is done by a North American, it means "No" or "I don't agree with you."

(A) Head shaking means different things in different cultures.

(B) The Europeans and the Asians use the same gesture for disagreement.

(C) The North Americans express disagreement by shaking their heads.

(D) Head shaking is the most common gesture to express agreement.

( ) 3. _____

For example, if a girl's name is Sandra, her friends might call her "Sandy." If a boy's name is Christopher, his parents might call him "Chris." Likewise, a man with the name Michael might be called "Mike" by his brothers or sisters.

(A) Not everyone has a pet name.

(B) It is not polite to call a person by his or her pet name.

(C) Some common pet names are "Sandy" and "Mike."

(D) A pet name is a shorter form of a person's first name and is usually used by the person's friends and family.

Writing II

Subject-Verb Agreement: Indefinite Pronouns

當不定代名詞當主詞時，一定要注意動詞的單複數。簡單的規則如下：

1. 僅用單數動詞：any, another, neither, something, nothing, much 等。
2. 僅用複數動詞：(a) few, both, many, several, (the) others 等。
3. 單複數皆有可能：all, most, some 等不定代名詞，如果 of 後面的名詞為可數，則動詞用複數；如果 of 後面的名詞為不可數，則動詞用單數。

Exercise: 在空格內填寫適當的動詞形式。

1. Mr. Li has three cars. One is black, another is red, and the other _____ (be) blue.

2. _____ (do) any of these buses go to the airport?

3. Andy has tried everything to lose weight, but nothing _____ (seem) to work.

4. Julie looked for a pen on her desk, but there _____ (be) not any.

5. "Something _____ (be) moving in the dark!" the girl cries.

6. Most of my friends _____ (live) in the same town as I do.

7. Jack and Chris are smart, but neither _____ (know) how to solve the math problem.

8. A few of Dr. Wang's students _____ (be) not in class today.

9. All of my money _____ (come) from my parents.

10. Many new dancers join the group, but only several of them _____ (be) males.

11. Two nurses work in the doctor's office, and both _____ (get) paid very well.

12. All of the jobs _____ (have) been taken by the new graduates this year.

13. Some TV shows are exciting, while others _____ (be) boring.

14. Much of the noise _____ (come) from the factory.

15. Most of the information _____ (be) valuable for the research project.

Advanced Reading I

 ## Business [1]Etiquette for Addressing Others

The business world has always [2]**valued** proper etiquette, so [3]**properly** addressing people is very important in creating good first impressions. Different countries and cultures will have very different [4]**customs** of doing this. That's why many companies even hire [5]**experts** to teach their employees how to communicate with people from other cultures, including using proper forms of address.

Nice to meet you, Mr. Jones.

Ms. Smith, this is my boss, Mr. Jones.

In America, formal forms of address are common for greeting someone for the first time. Usually, "Mr." (pronounced [ˋmɪstə]) is used for a man. When you are not sure if a woman is married, then use "Ms." (pronounced [ˋmɪz]) followed by the last name. Sometimes, you can also use "Dr." (pronounced [ˋdɑktə]) if that person holds a [6]**Ph.D.** Most Americans will quickly tell you that you are welcome to call them by their first names instead. If they are uncomfortable with these [7]**titles** and their first names, they will let you know what to call them.

[8]**Compared** with the Americans, the Japanese are very [9]**strict** about "proper" forms of address. There is a clear difference between a business and a personal relationship. In a business one, it is important to use "-san" (pronounced [san]) after a person's first name, last name, or full name. Only close friends or family members are allowed to call a person by his or her first name.

Using proper forms of address is very important in building a good business relationship. Learn and [10]**observe** the proper etiquette for addressing others in the country that you will be doing business in. You will be surprised how much it can do for you.

It's a pleasure to meet you, Yamada-san.

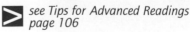

see Tips for Advanced Readings page 106

Advanced Reading II

Working with Foreign Cultures

No matter what culture you grew up in, it is always a [1]**challenge** to communicate and work with people from different cultures. This is especially true when you try to build a new business relationship. That's why it can be very valuable to learn about your business [2]**partner**'s culture.

First, the line between a "business" relationship and a "personal" relationship is not always [3]**cut and dried** in every culture. For example, in the U.S. and Europe, "business" usually comes first, and people pay little attention to personal matters. However, in Asia, it is common to begin a business relationship on a personal level. The best thing to do is: [4]**start out as** friends with your business partner, but always be prepared to get down to business.

Also, time is viewed very differently among cultures. In the U.S., being on time is very important. If you schedule a meeting for 2 p.m., be sure to arrive five or ten minutes early. Being late for over 15 minutes is considered [5]**rude**. Yet in Italy and Spain, things are different. Don't be surprised if your business partners arrive a little later than you expect. The best practice is to arrive on time, but be prepared to wait if necessary.

The idea of personal space is also different from culture to culture. In some countries, people prefer to be very close when they talk, while in others, it is the opposite. For example, in Japan, the U.S., and Europe, people keep at least an arm's [6]**length** during a conversation. They get uncomfortable if you stand very close to them. Yet in many [7]**Latin American** and [8]**Arabic** cultures, a short personal [9]**distance** is normal during a conversation. So, always make sure you follow the words of [10]**wisdom** when you interact with foreign partners: " [11]**When in Rome, do as the Romans do.**"

It is important to learn and understand that different cultures often do things differently, especially if you plan to work in [12]**international** business. Learning these differences will help you build good business relationships.

> *see Tips for Advanced Readings*
> *page 106*

5

10

15

20

25

30

Turn right at the corner.

🎧 Asking for and Giving Directions

Chris (C) is meeting up with one of his local friends, Natalie (N), at a coffee shop. He is asking her for directions on the cellphone.

C: Hey, Natalie, I just ¹**got off** the bus, but I don't see a coffee shop called Starlight.

N: You must have gotten off at the wrong stop. Tell me where you are now.

C: Umm.... I'm on Fifth Street between Second and Third ²**Avenue**—in front of a ³**bakery** called Suzie's.

N: Sounds like you really got off at the wrong stop.

C: I'm afraid so. Where should I go from here?

N: Don't worry. Go down to Third Avenue. Then turn to your right.

C: OK. That's easy.

N: ⁴**Continue straight** for two blocks. You'll see it on your left—across the street.

C: All right. I ⁵**get it** now. I'll be there in ten minutes.

Tips for You

1. get off　下車
2. avenue [ˋævəˏnju] *n.* 大街
3. bakery [ˋbekərɪ] *n.* 麵包店，糕餅店
4. continue straight　直走，直行
5. get it　明白，瞭解

🎧 *Listen to the conversations on the cellphone, and choose the correct answers.*

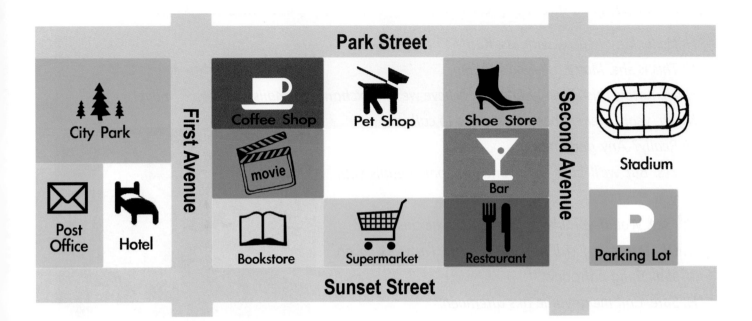

_____ 1. The woman is going to

_____.

(A) the supermarket

(B) the bookstore

(C) the bar

(D) the post office

_____ 3. The woman is going to

_____.

(A) the coffee shop

(B) the shoe store

(C) the restaurant

(D) the city park

_____ 2. The man can't find _____.

(A) the supermarket

(B) the bookstore

(C) the movie theater

(D) the pet shop

_____ 4. The man can't find _____.

(A) the city park

(B) the movie theater

(C) the bar

(D) the supermarket

Conversation & Useful Expressions II

🎧 Making Telephone Calls

1. *Henry (H) is calling Kathy Chen (K), an* ¹**editor** *at a* ²**publishing company**.

H: Hello. May I speak with Ms. Kathy Chen, please?

K: This is she. May I ask who's calling?

H: Hi, Kathy, this is Henry Parker. I believe we've ³**exchanged** emails about my ⁴**novel**.

K: Oh, yeah, I remember. I was going to call you.

H: Really? Any good news?

K: Yes. But we'll have to ⁵**work out** some details with you.

H: I see. Would you like to meet sometime this week?

K: OK. But...can I call you back later? I'm working on something right now.

H: Sure. Call me anytime this afternoon.

K: Great. I'll talk to you later. Have a nice day!

H: You, too! Bye!

2. *Chris (C) is calling his friend, Leo (L).*

C: Hi. This is Chris. Is Leo there?

L: Hi, Chris, what's up?

C: Nothing. I'm just calling to say hi.

L: Hey, thanks for calling. But I'm in the shower.

C: Oh, I'm sorry.

L: No problem. Let me call you back later, OK?

C: Sure. Talk to you later! Bye!

L: Bye, Chris.

Tips for You

1. editor [ˈɛdɪtɚ] *n.* 編輯
2. publish [ˈpʌblɪʃ] *v.* 出版
   publishing company　出版公司
3. exchange [ɪksˈtʃendʒ] *v.* (書信) 來往；交換
4. novel [ˈnɑvl̩] *n.* 小說
5. work out　讓⋯定案

Work in pairs and complete the following dialogues. Take turns playing the roles of the caller, and the person who answers the phone.

1. You are calling one of your classmates to see what he or she is doing.

> A: Hi, _____, please?
>
> B: Hi, _____.
>
> A: I am just calling to see _____.
>
> B: Well, I am working on a paper. Remember? The one that is ¹**due** tomorrow.
>
> A: I know. I've finished it. Is there anything I can help you with?
>
> B: Not really. I'm almost done here. But I have to get back to work now. Let me _____
> _____?

2. You are calling your best friend who you haven't seen for a long time. Ask your friend how he or she has been lately.

> A: Hi, _____?
>
> B: Hi, _____?
>
> A: I am just calling to see _____.
>
> B: Couldn't be better. _____
>
> A: Me, too. Thanks _____.
>
> B: Hey, don't say that. You're my best friend. Of course, I'd love to talk to you ²**from time to time.**

3. You ³**applied** for a job three days ago. You are calling the manager, Mr./Ms. Lu, and see if what he or she has received your ⁴**résumé**.

> A: Hi, _____, please?
>
> B: _____ May I _____?
>
> A: Hi, Mr./Ms. Lu, this is _____. I applied for the job of ⁵**sales representative** several days ago. I am just calling to _____
> _____.
>
> B: I have. But I am still ⁶**reviewing** it. Let me call you back in a week. Is that OK?
>
> A: Sure. You can call me anytime next week.

Tips for You

1. due [dju] *n.* 到期的
2. from time to time 偶爾
3. apply [ə`plaɪ] *v.* 應徵；申請
4. résumé [`rɛzəme] *n.* 履歷（表）
5. sales representative 業務代表
6. review [rɪ`vju] *v.; n.* 審查，檢閱；複習

Short Reading

Traffic on ¹Venus and ²Mars

A husband and wife are driving to another town to watch a play. They get lost on the way. The wife wants to stop and ask for directions, but her husband, who is the driver, ³**refuses** to do so. By the time he finds out how to get there, the play has started, and the ⁴**couple** has stopped—speaking with each other.

This ⁵**scenario** shows a ⁶**typical** difference between men and women: men want to appear strong and in no need of help, while women like to work together. The lost-in-the-car scenario is so common that it has become a cultural ⁷**cliché** in the United States. The trouble is, it isn't true.

According to a ⁸**survey** of 2,000 people by the ⁹**American Automobile Association** (AAA), when men drivers get lost, they ask for directions 34 percent of the time. The same survey also shows that when women find themselves in the same situation, they ask for directions just 37 percent of the time. The difference is not great between men and women.

So why do people believe that most men would rather drive in circles than ask for directions? The AAA discovers that 78 percent of the time, the man does the driving when a couple is in the car. In other words, because men drive more often, they refuse to ask for directions more often, too.

The AAA also discovers that most couples wait less than a half hour before asking for directions, though a few drivers of both sexes drive around for four hours before asking for help. While many men might prefer sports to romance and beer to good wine, they are not really so bad about asking for directions— at least no worse than women are. So, if women lived on Venus and men lived on Mars, the traffic on one of the two planets would not be much better or worse than on the other.

Tips for You

1. Venus [ˋvinəs] *n.* 金星
2. Mars [mɑrz] *n.* 火星
3. refuse [rɪˋfjuz] *v.* 拒絕
4. couple [ˋkʌpl̩] *n.* 夫妻，情侶
5. scenario [sɪˋnɛrɪ͵o] *n.* 可能的狀況
6. typical [ˋtɪpɪkl̩] *n.* 典型的

7. cliché [kliˋʃe] *n.* 陳腔濫調
   clichéd [kliˋʃed] *adj.* 陳腔濫調的
8. survey [ˋsɝve] *n.* 調查；[sɝˋve] *v.* 調查
9. American Automobile Association
   (the ~) 美國汽車協會
   automobile [ˋɔtəmə͵bɪl] *n.* 汽車
   association [ə͵sosɪˋeʃən] *n.* 協會；關連

I. Choose the correct answer to each of the following questions based on the reading.

( ) 1. What is the main idea of the reading?

(A) Men ask for directions less often because they do the driving 78 percent of the time.

(B) It is not true that women ask for directions much more often than men do.

(C) Most couples drive around for more than 4 hours before asking for help.

(D) Few drivers drive in circles less than 2 hours before asking for directions.

( ) 2. Which of the following statements is true?

(A) When men get lost, they ask for directions 37 percent of the time.

(B) When women get lost, they ask for directions 37 percent of the time.

(C) When men get lost, they don't ask for directions 63 percent of the time.

(D) When women get lost, they don't ask for directions 66 percent of the time.

( ) 3. According to the American Automobile Association, when a couple is in the car, the man is the driver _____ percent of the time.

(A) 37   (B) 34   (C) 67   (D) 78

II. Check (✓) the ideas that are included in the reading.

☐ 1. A survey of 2,000 people by the AAA shows that men want to appear strong.

☐ 2. Men refuse to ask for directions more often because they drive more often.

☐ 3. The lost-in-the-car scenario shows that it is better for women to live on Venus.

☐ 4. The AAA discovers that most couples wait for less than half an hour before asking for directions.

☐ 5. The traffic on Mars is much better than that on Venus.

☐ 6. Men drive more often because they own the car most of the time.

☐ 7. Venus and Mars are the largest planets that move around the sun.

Review: Topic Sentences/Choose a Topic Sentence

由於主題句代表了全段的中心思想，因此其中的概念應該足以涵蓋每個段落中的句子。

Three students are in the classroom.

1. One of them is Ron.

2. Another is Tim.

3. The other is Jessica.

Exercise: 從下列句子中，選出足以涵蓋其他三個句子的主題句。

(　　) 1. (A) Women talk a lot more than men.

(B) Women are not as strong as men.

(C) Men ask for directions less often than women.

(D) Women and men are stereotyped to be different in many ways.

(　　) 2. (A) There is a lot we can do to stay healthy.

(B) Exercise at least for 30 minutes every day.

(C) Stay away from junk food.

(D) Remember to get enough sleep.

(　　) 3. (A) The more popular products will be sold out by then.

(B) Every shop or department store will be full of shoppers.

(C) Don't wait until last minute to do your Christmas shopping.

(D) It can be difficult to get the shopping list ready in a hurry.

Writing II

Review: Subject-Verb Agreement: Indefinite Pronouns

除了上一課所列的幾個不定代名詞 (indefinite pronouns)，僅用單數動詞的不定代名詞還有：anyone, anything, each, none, someone, anybody, somebody 等。

Exercise: 在空格內填寫適當的動詞形式。

1. Both of Ian's parents ＿＿＿＿＿＿ (*look*) very young—even in their seventies.

2. Judy has three bothers. One is Sam, another is David, and the other ＿＿＿＿＿＿ (*be*) Kent.

3. Most of Richard's friends ＿＿＿＿＿＿ (*know*) his nickname.

4. Mr. Ellison makes sure that each of his children ＿＿＿＿＿＿ (*learn*) to do housework.

5. Forty students are taking English 101 from Dr. Wu, and several ＿＿＿＿＿＿ (*seem*) to have trouble turning in assignments on time.

6. Much of Sarah's time ＿＿＿＿＿＿ (*have*) been spent on her work.

7. In that old village, all of the water ＿＿＿＿＿＿ (*come*) from the river nearby.

8. None of the books on the shelf ＿＿＿＿＿＿ (*interest*) me.

9. During the job interview, the manager usually asks if there ＿＿＿＿＿＿ (*be*) anything the applicant wants to know about the company.

10. "Somebody ＿＿＿＿＿＿ (*be*) waiting for you in your office," Mr. Tan's secretary told him.

11. Seven new employees start working in the company today, and some ＿＿＿＿＿＿ (*need*) additional training.

12. Dan has two computers, but neither ＿＿＿＿＿＿ (*work*).

13. Several of the employees ＿＿＿＿＿＿ (*ask*) for a pay raise, and the boss approves it.

14. James gets angry if any of his children ＿＿＿＿＿＿ (*come*) home after 11 p.m.

15. "Take a message for me if anyone ＿＿＿＿＿＿ (*call*)," Ms. Lin told her assistant.

31

Talking Without ¹Walking on Thin Ice

There are differences in men's and women's communication styles. Learning about them can be very helpful—both professionally and ²**personally**.

5   When it comes to communication styles, men usually ³**focus** on ⁴**information**. This may include telling people what to do or asking questions. That's why men avoid small talk during meetings and put all their

10 attention on solving problems. For example, at the beginning of business meetings, men typically like to talk about facts and get down to work right away. This type of communication focuses on "information"

15 and "problem-solving."

    On the other hand, women like to focus on creating a sense of " ⁵**agreement**" among members of a group. That often includes sharing feelings and expressing

20 opinions. For example, at the beginning of a business meeting, women typically want to find out how everyone feels and thinks about the problems. Also, in the process of making decisions, women generally like to make sure that everyone is ⁶**involved**. 25 This style of communication focuses on "sharing" and "feelings."

    These differences in communication styles can cause misunderstandings between the two ⁷**genders**. Sometimes, 30 women complain that men are " ⁸**insensitive**" and care only about facts, not feelings. On the other hand, men may feel that women are ⁹**unproductive** and waste lots of time on feelings, not facts. 35

    Communicating with members of the opposite sex is not as difficult as we think. All it takes is the understanding and acceptance of gender differences—in communication styles, that is. 40

> *see Tips for Advanced Readings page 106*

🎧 Equality in the ¹Workplace: Much Needs to Be Done

The ²**Equal Rights Amendment** has been a part of the American ³**Constitution** for over 85 years. One of the main reasons for it was to make sure that men and women would be treated equally.

However, the Equal Rights Amendment has failed to push the American society to treat men and women equally in the workplace. Today, men still hold most of the high level ⁴**positions** in the U.S., such as ⁵**political** and business leaders; women still don't get paid as well as those men who hold the same positions in the workplace. Studies have shown that the average ⁶**salary** for women is about 23.5 percent lower than that for men. Also, in America's top companies, women ⁷**make up** only 16 percent of corporate executives, and 2 percent of chief executive officers.

One can't help but wonder why such inequalities still ⁸**exisit** in the U.S.—despite the fact that the Equal Rights Amendment has been in place for over 85 years. There could be a number of causes for this. One of them is the traditional belief that it is men's nature to be ⁹**aggressive** and strong, and so it makes them better leaders than women. On the other hand, women are wrongly believed to be weak and emotional, and so they should hold positions of support. Though unfair and wrong, these gender ¹⁰**stereotypes** have caused many women to believe that they don't have the same abilities as men do to be leaders.

For gender inequalities to disappear from the workplace, every member of the society must recognize and ¹¹**act upon** one simple fact: a person's gender does NOT decide what he or she can or cannot do at work. Though the fact is simple, much needs to be done before everyone comes to believe it.

> *see Tips for Advanced Readings page 106*

The meeting is scheduled for Friday.

❶ take a rain check on... 擇期再…	❺ at 5:30 sharp 五點半整	❾ no-show 爽約；爽約的人
❷ be postponed until/to... 延後到…	❻ first come, first served 先到先服務	❿ walk-in 未經預約而來的
❸ cancel 取消	❼ on time 準時	⓫ (make an) appointment (安排) 約會
❹ move...to... 把…的時間改到…	❽ schedule 預定、安排時間	

(18) Making Appointments

1. *Laura (L) is calling a hair salon to make an appointment with her hairstylist. A [1]receptionist (R) is speaking with her on the phone.*

R: Venus Beauty Salon, may I help you?

L: Yes. This is Laura Parker. I'd like to make an appointment with Gloria.

R: Hi, Ms. Parker. Hold on, please. Let me get the schedule book.

   (a few seconds later)

R: Thank you for waiting. When would you like to come in?

L: Saturday afternoon. Three o'clock. And I'd like to get a [2]**perm** that day.

R: Let me see.... I'm sorry. That [3]**time slot** has been taken. What about four o'clock?

L: That will be fine. Put me down for four o'clock.

R: So, that's four o'clock. Saturday afternoon. Right?

L: That's correct.

R: All right. I'll see you on Saturday then.

2. *Chris (C) has a toothache. He's calling a [4]**dental clinic** to make an appointment. An office [5]assitant (A) answers the phone.*

C: Hi, this is Chris Parker. I am calling to see if Dr. Yu is [6]**available** this afternoon.

A: Hold on, please.... Oh, I'm sorry. Her schedule is full today.

C: [7]**Goodness!** My toothache is killing me! Would you please [8]**squeeze** me in?

A: Let me see what I can do.

   (a few seconds later)

A: Hi. I just asked Dr. Yu. She'll stay [9]**after-hours** to see you.

C: Really? Thank you!

A: [10]**Don't mention it.** Your name, please.

C: Chris Parker. C-H-R-I-S P-A-R-K-E-R.

A: Got it. So, come in at 5 o'clock sharp.

C: I will. Thank you for your help.

Tips for You

1. receptionist [rɪˋsɛptʃənɪst] *n.* 接待人員
2. perm [pɝm] *n.* 燙頭髮
3. time slot 時段
4. dental clinic 牙科診所
   dentist [ˋdɛntɪst] *n.* 牙醫
5. assistant [əˋsɪstənt] *n.* 助理

6. available [əˋveləbl] *adj.* 有時間的；可得的
7. Goodness! [ˋgudnɪs] 天啊！
8. squeeze...in 為…擠出時間
9. after-hours [ˋæftɚˏaurz] *adv.* 在下班之後
10. Don't mention it. 別客氣

You'll hear four people calling a clinic to make appointments. Complete the appointment cards below based on the conversations.

1.

Name	Jonathan Yang
Day	_____
Time	_____ a.m.
Doctor	Dr. Smith

3.

Name	Samuel Su
Day	_____
Time	_____ p.m.
Doctor	Dr. Lin

2.

Name	Betty Kim
Day	_____
Time	_____ a.m.
Doctor	Dr. Smith

4.

Name	John Chen
Day	_____
Time	_____ p.m.
Doctor	Dr. Lin

UNIT 3 **Conversation & Useful Expressions II**

🎧 ⓴ Expressing Preferences for ¹Objects, Activities, Etc.

1. *Henry (H) is shopping for a shirt in a department store. Laura (L) is with him.*

L : What do you think about this shirt?

H: Umm.... Honestly, I'd ²**prefer** a darker color **to** baby blue.

L : But it looks great on you.

H: Laura, anything in baby blue just doesn't ³**turn** me **on**.

L : Fine. What about this one? It's dark blue.

H: That looks better. It'll go with my new ⁴**khakis**.

L : I'm not so sure about that. But, whatever turns you on, dear.

2. *Chris (C) is inviting his friend, Michael (M), to a basketball game.*

C: Hey, Michael, do you have any plans for Saturday?

M: Not yet. Why?

C: I have two tickets for a basketball game. Want to come along?

M: Well, basketball is ⁵**not my cup of tea**.

C: Why not? I personally ⁶**get a kick out of** going to a basketball game.

M: I don't know why you ⁷**have a thing for** basketball. But I just don't.

C: Alright then. Looks like I have to find someone else to go with me.

M: Sorry, Chris. I ⁸**'d rather** watch TV **than** go to a basketball game.

🏷️ Tips for You

1. object [ˋɑbdʒɪkt] *n.* 物品
2. prefer A to B　喜歡 A 勝過於 B
3. turn someone on　讓某人感興趣
4. khaki [ˋkɑkɪ] *n. (usua. pl.)* 卡其褲

5. not someone's cup of tea　不是某人喜歡的事物
6. get a kick out of　從…獲得刺激、快感
7. have a thing for/about...　莫名地喜歡…
8. would rather...than...　寧可…也不…

38

Work in pairs and complete the following dialogues.

1. You got two dogs from a pet shop last week. Now you want to give away one of them to your friend.

> A: Look! I've got two puppies from the pet shop. Don't you just love them?
>
> B: Not really. _____
>
> A: You like cats better than dogs? [1] **How come?**
>
> B: Well, the idea of keeping a dog just _____, especially a puppy.
>
> A: Well, all you need to do is train it—and have some patience.
>
> B: Train it? You mean [2] **potty training**? Goodness! [3] **You are out of your mind.**

2. You are shopping for a new bike. One of your friends is with you in the bicycle shop.

> A: How about that one in the corner? It's black.
>
> B: It's too dark for me. _____
>
> A: Lighter colors? Such as...?
>
> B: Red or yellow. Do they have bikes in red or yellow?
>
> A: Red or yellow? Listen, I don't know why _____.
>   But, _____. [4] **Go for** that one in red then.
>
> B: Yeah, now, you are talking.

3. You just bought some stinky tofu. Now, you are asking one of your roommates if he or she would like to have some.

> A: Hey, I just got some stinky tofu. Do you want to [5] **have a bite**?
>
> B: [6] **Yikes.** _____
>
> A: Die? Oh, come on, it's not that bad.
>
> B: Yes, it is! It smells bad, and it tastes bad. I don't get it. Why do you _____
>   _____?
>
> A: Well, you like to play computer games, and I don't. Why? It's just _____
>   _____. Get it now?

Tips for You

1. How come?　為什麼？
2. potty training　(給小孩或寵物的) 便溺訓練，
   如廁訓練
3. You are out of your mind.　你瘋了
4. go for　選擇
5. have a bite　吃一口
6. yikes [jaɪks] *interj.* 呀！(表示受到驚嚇或驚訝)

From "Time" to "Time"

People in different areas of the world have different [1]**concepts** of what time really means. For example, in Latin America and the Arab World, time is [2]**flexible**. Schedules and appointments are adjusted to meet the needs of people. However, in Europe and North America, people adjust themselves to meet the needs of schedules and appointments.

5 　People in Europe and North America believe that time is money. And [3]**indeed**, it is for them in many ways. For example, many doctors require appointments. They believe that an appointment is not only a matter of [4]**courtesy** but also a matter of money. Since only one person can be scheduled for a specific time, they expect people to show up for their appointments.

10 　Many [5]**professionals**, such as lawyers and business executives, take this [6]**notion** of time and money very seriously. Indeed, if a person misses a scheduled appointment entirely, he or she will typically be charged for the missed appointment. Even though no services are received, the person must still pay. Further, there are stories in the West about professionals refusing to see [7]**clients** who arrived only a few minutes past the scheduled time.

15 　The [8]**Brazilians**, however, have a different concept of "time." Time, in their daily lives, is viewed with flexibility. For example, if a class begins at 10:00 in the morning, students usually do NOT arrive in the classroom at 10:00 sharp. In fact, they are usually allowed to come in at 10:30 without being considered "late." Why? Because it is acceptable in their culture.

　Each culture has its own way of viewing time, schedules, and appointments, and each
20 has its own reasons for doing so. As a result, it is best to consider a person's cultural [9]**background** before [10]**judging** him or her. And of course, next time you make a doctor's appointment in the United States, be sure to show up, and show up on time. If you can't [11]**make it to** the appointment, at least give a 24-hour notice [12]**in advance**. Otherwise, you may find yourself paying for services you've never received!

Tips for You

1. concept [`kɑnsɛpt] *n.* 概念
2. flexible [`flɛksəbl̩] *adj.* 具彈性的
   flexibility [ˌflɛksə`bɪlətɪ] *n.* 彈性
3. indeed [ɪn`did] *adv.* 的確
4. courtesy [`kɝtəsɪ] *n.* 禮貌
5. professional [prə`fɛʃənl̩] *n.*; *adj.*
   專業人員；專業的
6. notion [`noʃən] *n.* 觀念，看法

7. client [`klaɪənt] *n.* 顧客，客戶
8. Brazilian [brə`zɪljən] *n.*; *adj.* 巴西人；巴西的
   Brazil [brə`zɪl] *n.* 巴西
9. background [`bæk͵graʊd] *n.* 背景
10. judge [dʒʌdʒ] *v.*; *n.* 論斷；法官
11. make it to 趕上，趕到
12. in advance 事先地

I. *Choose the correct answer to each of the following questions base on the reading.*

( ) 1. The _____ view time with flexibility.

    (A) Americans   (B) Brazilians   (C) Asians   (D) Europeans

( ) 2. According to the reading, professionals in America and Europe _____.

    (A) charge their clients if they fail to show up for appointments

    (B) allow their clients to arrive late without charging them anything

    (C) take the notion of time very flexibly

    (D) believe being on time is only a matter of courtesy

( ) 3. Which of the following statements is true?

    (A) The Brazilians always show up for appointments at the scheduled time.

    (B) The Europeans allow their students to arrive in classrooms late.

    (C) Showing up for appointments at scheduled times is important in the Arab world.

    (D) Some professionals in the West refuse to see clients who are a few minutes late for their appointments.

II. *Check (✓) the ideas that are included in the reading.*

☐ 1. Flexibility in viewing appointments and schedules is not uncommon in the Arab World.

☐ 2. In the U.S., if you can't make it to an appointment, be sure to give a week's notice in advance.

☐ 3. In the West, business executives or lawyers can never refuse to see their clients who arrive after scheduled times.

☐ 4. Each culture has its own way of viewing time, schedules, and appointments.

☐ 5. Most Latin Americans don't take schedules and appointments very seriously.

☐ 6. In Europe and North America, a person is usually scheduled for a specific time.

☐ 7. In North America, schedules and appointments are adjusted to meet the needs of people.

General or Specific

在段落或文章裡的句子，其含意有廣度上的差別。內容上較為廣泛的 (general)，通常適合當作主題句。相對地，內容較為針對特定 (specific) 細節的，則通常用來支持或證明主題句裡的含意。

Exercise: 下列各組句子中，將較有可能是主題句的以 G (general) 標示，而較有可能用來支持或證明主題句的，以 S (specific) 表示。

1. _____ In Brazil, it is common for students to arrive in classrooms late.

   _____ The Latin Americans view time with flexibility.

2. _____ People are allowed to be late in certain areas of the world.

   _____ In the Philippines, appointments can be met 30 minutes after the scheduled time.

3. _____ Pet owners are usually faced with problems when it's time for a vacation.

   _____ Pets are hardly welcome in hotels or restaurants.

4. _____ There are a few tips for managing time better.

   _____ Allow "more than enough" time for traffic when scheduling an appointment.

5. _____ Taipei is an hour ahead of Tokyo.

   _____ Everyone in international business should know there are time differences.

Use Parallelism Correctly

1. 句子中，當兩個平行的字、詞、片語、句子等，是用連接詞結合起來時，稱之為「平行結構」(parallelism)。因此，連接詞兩端的架構要對等，如：名詞接名詞，動詞接動詞等。
2. 常用的連接詞有兩種：
   A. 對等連接詞：and、but、or、yet 等。
   B. 相關連接詞：「both...and...」、「not... but...」、「either...or...」、「neither...nor...」、「not only...but also...」等。

Exercise: 將下列題目中以底線標示的錯誤部分，改正在該題的空白欄。

1. Arriving in classrooms late is unacceptable in both Europe and North Americans.

   _____

2. In Latin America, showing up for an appointment after a scheduled time is not wrong but viewed with acceptance.

   _____

3. Mary doesn't want to be a model but teach English.

   _____

4. Taking notes and to review notes are two important learning strategies.

   _____

5. Learning a second language takes not only time but also patient.

   _____

6. Jack felt neither anger nor sad when his girlfriend left him.

   _____

7. When you get lost, the best thing to do is either getting a map or to ask for directions.

   _____

8. Call Mr. Rogers on his cellphone or leaving a message to his secretary.

   _____

9. Mr. Donaldson's children have to follow strictly yet reasonable rules at home.

   _____

10. The police tried to find out both how and at what time the two travelers were murdered.

    _____

The Secretary Is [1]on Guard

All around the world, [2]**overworked** business executives depend on their assistants, or secretaries, to help them. Among
5 their other [3]**duties**, secretaries are usually the people who manage their bosses' schedules and appointments. So, if you want to make an appointment
10 with a business executive, you will probably have to arrange it through his or her secretary.

Secretaries in different cultures see their jobs in
15 different ways. For example, in America, it is considered important for a secretary to be friendly, and to make callers and visitors feel welcome. If you call to make an appointment with an American business
20 executive, his or her secretary will try to be [4]**as** helpful **as possible** and greet you warmly when you arrive for your appointment.

In France, however, there is a different culture for secretaries. They see themselves
25 as their bosses' [5]**protectors**, and try to keep outside people away because they will waste the executive's time. So if you want to make an appointment with a French business executive, first you have to make it through
30 the "secretary [6]**barrier**."

If you call to speak to the executive in France, the secretary will not let you. He or 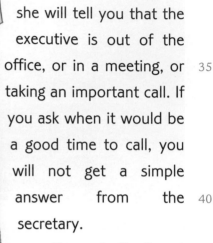 she will tell you that the executive is out of the office, or in a meeting, or 35 taking an important call. If you ask when it would be a good time to call, you will not get a simple answer from the 40 secretary.

If you do finally get an appointment, the secretary might make you wait for a long time 45 before you can start your meeting. And if you are not important enough, he or she will also [7]**interrupt** your meeting so that the executive can take phone calls. A secretary 50 may even remind the executive of other appointments that are starting soon, so that you have to end your meeting early.

Luckily, [8]**voice mail** and e-mail have made it easier to [9]**contact** business 55 executives [10]**directly**, without talking to the secretary. This may finally mean the end of the "secretary barrier" in France — [11]**unless** the executives ask their secretaries to answer their voice mail and e-mails for 60 them!

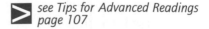 *see Tips for Advanced Readings page 107*

My Time or Your Time?

Different cultures view time in different ways. Some cultures, known as [1]**monochronic** cultures, place a great deal of importance on time. Daily schedules are strictly followed, appointments are made far in advance, and people are expected to always arrive on time. Other cultures are [2]**polychronic**, which means that they view time more flexibly. In these cultures, greater emphasis is placed on relationships, which means that family [3]**obligations** 5 are expected to come first. Being on time is not as important, and plans are never kept unchanged.

Some examples of monochromatic countries are Asian countries, the United States, and some European countries. For instance, in Korea, it is rude to cancel or be late for an appointment, even a social [4]**gathering** with friends or family. The United States is a little 10 less strict, but punctuality is still important. Although being a few minutes late for a social [5]**engagement** is acceptable and sometimes even expected, Americans are expected to be on time or a few minutes early to all other appointments.

Polychromatic countries include many Latin American and Arab countries. For example, Mexico has a very relaxed daily schedule where everyone usually takes an afternoon break of several hours, known as a *siesta*, to eat a [6]**leisurely** late lunch and spend time with family. It is generally expected that family [7]**responsibilities** come before business obligations or other appointments, making punctuality a goal rather than a necessity. Likewise, in [8]**Saudi Arabia**, [9]**hospitality** is very important, and [10]**therefore** appointments are often made for 20 a general time of day, if at all. However, this flexibility does not include the time for religious prayers.

As you can see, the meaning of time [11]**varies** widely between cultures. Some countries 25 place a high importance on setting and keeping a schedule, while other countries are more concerned about family and relationships than being on time. When you make an appointment or schedule a social gathering with friends from other countries, keep in mind that your "time" is not necessarily their "time." 30

▶ *see Tips for Advanced Readings page 107*

45

I can't stand it anymore!

1. hug 擁抱
2. close up/up close 靠近
3. a kiss (on the cheek) 吻 (臉頰)
4. hand in hand 手牽手
5. pinch/squeeze 捏，擰
6. nose rubbing 摩擦鼻子
7. a pat on the back/ head 摸頭；拍背
8. keep a distance 保持距離
9. head to head 頭對頭
10. shove 用力推
11. put an arm around one's shoulder 與…勾肩
12. tap one on the arm/ shoulder 輕拍肩膀／手臂
13. grab one on the arm 抓某人的手臂

(26) Complaining About Personal Proximity

1. Natalie (N) has just arrived at Chris's home for dinner. Chris's father greets her with a hug. Now, Natalie is complaining to Chris (C) about the hug.

N: *Did you see that? Your dad just hugged me.*

C: *Yeah. And...? Anything* [1] **wrong with** *that?*

N: *Uhh...I'm just not comfortable with hugs.*

C: *Hey,* [2] **lighten up**. *It's not a big deal.*

N: *Well, I don't like it when people hug me.*

C: *But I've seen you hug your best friend, Judy.*

N: *Judy is a girl, and your father is a guy.*

C: *Oh, that's right. What if my dad gives you a* [3] **handshake** *next time?*

N: *I'll be more comfortable with that.*

C: *No problem. I'll tell my dad about this.*

2. Natalie (N) sees Chris (C) in the library. She goes up to say hi.

N: *Hey, what's up, Chris? (tapping Chris on the head)*

C: *Nothing much.*

N: *I am here to study for a test.*

C: *Uhh...Natalie, I hate to bring this up, but....*

N: [4] **What's wrong**, *Chris?*

C: *Would you please stop tapping me on the head? I hate it when people do that to me.*

N: *I thought we were friends.*

C: *We are. But....*

N: *What is it then? Anthing you want to tell me?*

C: *Goodness, Natalie. It's just* [5] **annoying**, [6] **period**.

Tips for You

1. wrong with　有問題
2. lighten up　放輕鬆點
3. handshake [`hænd͵ʃek] *n.* 握手
4. What's wrong (with...)?　…有問題嗎？

5. annoying [ə`nɔɪɪŋ] *adj.* 令人厭煩的
   annoy [ə`nɔɪ] *v.* 使…感到厭煩
6. period [`pɪrɪəd] *interj.* 反正就是這樣
   period [`pɪrɪəd] *n.* 時期；句號

Listen to the conversations, and choose the correct answers.

_____ 1. The woman doesn't like it when
_____.
(A) she is trying to be friendly
(B) Billy rubs his shoulder on hers
(C) she is friendly but Billy is not
(D) Billy puts his arm around her
     shoulder

_____ 2. Rick likes to _____ when
he says hi to the woman.
(A) ask the woman to tap him on
     the hand
(B) tap the woman on the head
(C) tap the woman on her hand
(D) ask the woman to tap him on
     the head

_____ 3. The daughter doesn't like it when
her father _____.
(A) hugs her friends in front of her
(B) hugged her when she was a kid
(C) hugs her in front of her friends
(D) hugged her friends when she
     was a kid

_____ 4. The man's wife likes to
_____.
(A) be pinched on the arm
(B) pinch him on his arm
(C) be pinched in his arms
(D) pinch herself on the arm

_____ 5. The waiter _____.
(A) tapped the woman on the head
(B) tapped the man on the head
(C) tapped his own daughter on
     the head
(D) tapped the man's daughter on
     the head

_____ 6. The man doens't like it
_____.
(A) when people talk to him up
     close
(B) when his best friends hate
     stinky tofu
(C) when his best friends live close
     to him
(D) when he has to close the door

🎧 Complaining About Personal Questions

1. *Laura (L) has just met Kevin (K) in a* ¹**yoga** *class. They are having a chat.*

K : *So, you are from* ²**the States**?

L : *Yes. I moved here with my family several months ago.*

K : *And you moved here because...?*

L : *Oh, I moved here for my job.*

K : *Your job? Wow, that sounds like a "good" job.*

L : *Well, I like it. That's the most important thing.*

K : *How much do they pay you?*

L : *Kevin, I don't feel comfortable talking about it.*

K : *Why? It's not a big deal, is it?*

L : *Yes, it is. We've just met, and I'd rather* ³**keep** *it* **to myself**.

2. *Katrina (K), an* ⁴**Australian**, *is one of Chris's friends. She is complaining to him about the guy she went out with yesterday.*

K : *I can't believe it!*

C : *What's wrong? Look at you. You're all upset.*

K : *It's the guy I had a* ⁵**date** *with yesterday.*

C : *Was he late for the date or what?*

K : *No. But he asked me how old I was.*

C : *Wow, no wonder you are so* ⁶**upset**.

K : *I told him, "Hey, I'd rather not talk about it." And he said I was too* ⁷**uptight**.

C : *You know what? Here, people are used to talking about their* ⁸**signs of the Chinese zodiac**. *So, they need to know when you were born.*

K : *Really? But isn't it too personal to talk about?*

C : *Maybe that's what you should have told the guy yesterday.*

Tips for You

1. yoga [ˋjogə] *n.* 瑜珈
2. the States (= the U.S.A.) 美國
3. keep...to oneself 不告訴別人某事
4. Australian [ɔˋstreljən] *n.* 澳洲人
   Australia [ɔˋstreljə] *n.* 澳洲
5. date [det] *n.* 約會；約會的人
6. upset [ʌpˋsɛt] *adj.* 心煩的
7. uptight [ˋʌpˋtaɪt] *adj.* 過於嚴謹的；焦慮的
8. signs of the Chinese zodiac 生肖
   zodiac [ˋzodɪˏæk] *n.* 黃道帶

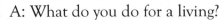

Work in pairs and complete each of the dialogues.

1

A: What do you do for a living?

B: I work as a ¹**general manager** at a ²**software** company.

A: Wow, the pay must be really good. How much do they pay you?

B: _____

A: Why?_____, is it?

B: Yes, it is. We've just met, and I don't feel comfortable talking about my ³**salary**.

2

A: So, you said your son is picking you up? Why not your husband?

B: Uh.... We don't live together.

A: Really? So, you two are ⁴**divorced** or ⁵**separated**?

B: It's _____.

A: I understand. _____

B: Yes. Thank you for being very understanding.

3

A: You said you went to see the doctor yesterday?

B: Yeah. I did.

A: What's wrong?

B: Uh.... _____

A: Oh, I'm sorry. This is something _____

_____. I shouldn't have asked.

B: Anyway, thank you for asking. I think I'll be fine.

Tips for You

1. general manager　總經理

2. software [`sɔft͵wɛr] *n.* 軟體

3. salary [`sælərɪ] *n.* 薪水

4. divorced [də`vɔrst] *adj.* 離婚的

　 divorce [də`vɔrs] *v.; n.* 與…離婚；離婚

5. separated [`sɛpə͵retɪd] *adj.* 分居

　 separate [`sɛpə͵ret] *v.* 分居；分開

Beyond Words

Doing business around the world is not just about attending meetings and visiting different countries. It is also about understanding and following different cultural patterns of communication. Do you know more than 70 percent of our daily communication is [1]**conducted** [2]**nonverbally**? This just tells you how important nonverbal communication is. If you work in international business, the following two aspects of nonverbal communication
5
can easily determine whether you will be able to close business deals with clients from other cultures.

The first is [3]**eye contact**. If you are speaking with people from North America and Latin America [4]**in person**, remember to have direct eye contact with them. If you fail to do so, they would think that you are hiding something from them or not paying attention. However, if you look at an Asian in the eye for a long time during a business meeting, he or she would consider you very rude. This could [5]**lead to** your failure to close a deal with
15
that person.

In addition, the amount of personal space that an [6]**individual** requires also differs across cultures. This time, Latin Americans do not [7]**see eye to eye with** North Americans. In Latin America, friendly physical contact is common, and gestures like shaking hands, or patting someone on the back are signs of friendliness. However, to North Americans, as well as Asians, a 2-foot distance is necessary for both sides to feel comfortable, especially in a business setting.

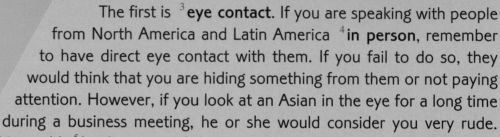

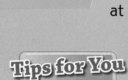

In order to close business deals with international partners, you should learn how they conduct nonverbal communication [8]**in advance**. You can [9]**surf the Internet**, ask a local friend, or observe local people's behavior to find answers for yourself. Maybe your next deal will be successfully closed simply because you keep the right distance and look at your clients in the way that makes them feel comfortable and respected.

Tips for You

1. conduct [kən`dʌkt] *v.* 進行，執行
2. nonverbally [,nɑn`vɝblɪ] *adv.* 非言語上地
   nonverbal [,nɑn`vɝbl] *adj.* 非言語上的
   verbal [`vɝbl] *adj.* 言語上的
3. eye contact   眼對眼接觸
4. in person   親自地

5. lead to   造成
6. individual [,ɪndə`vɪdʒʊəl] *n.*; *adj.* 個人；個別的
7. see eye to eye with...   同意…的看法
8. in advance   事前，事先
9. surf the Internet   在電腦網路上搜尋

I. *Based on the reading, mark each of the following statements with T (True) or F (False).*

_____ 1. Asians are used to having direct eye contact when they have conversations.

_____ 2. Surfing the Internet is the only way to learn how nonverbal communication is conducted in different cultures.

_____ 3. To Latin Americans, patting a person on the back is a friendly gesture.

_____ 4. Latin Americans are used to avoiding direct eye contact during conversations.

_____ 5. Asians need at least a 2-foot distance to feel comfortable with those who they have conversations with.

II. *Choose the correct answers.*

(　) 1. According to the reading, more than 70 percent of our _____ is conducted _____.

    (A) nonverbal communication; with gestures

    (B) daily communication; verbally

    (C) daily communication; nonverbally

    (D) verbal communication; in English

(　) 2. The two aspects of nonverbal communication mentioned in the reading are _____ and _____.

    (A) personal space; physical contact   (B) personal space; gestures

    (C) eye contact; paying attention   (D) eye contact; personal space

(　) 3. North Americans _____ those who they speak with.

    (A) avoid direct eye contact with

    (B) are used to physical contact with

    (C) give direct eye contact to

    (D) keep a 2-meter distance with

Review: General or Specific

如前一課所提及的，內容較為廣泛的句子，通常適合當作主題句；而內容較為針對特定 (specific) 細節的句子，則通常用來支持或證明主題句裡的含意。主題句常出現在段落的前方，以提示讀者全段的大綱；支持主題句的句子，則通常在段落的其他位置。

Exercise: 將句子填入段落中適當的位置。答題時，請將代表各句子的字母 (A、B) 填入段落中的空格。

> A. In addition, politics, religion, and sex are taboo topics of conversation in some cultures, but not in others.
> B. Different cultures have different ideas of what people should or shouldn't talk about.

1. _____ For example, in some cultures it is very rude to ask an adult female how old she is in a casual conversation. _____

> A. Smiles are important in bringing people together and making friends.
> B. Those who smile a lot are usually more popular than those who don't smile often.

2. _____ When you smile, you are actually helping people feel comfortable and easy around you. Also, a friendly smile sends a clear message: I am not dangerous to you. _____ This makes sense because we all want to be around friendly people.

Review: Use Parallelism Correctly

除了上一課所提到的原則，使用平行結構的句子中，如果主詞是用 or 或 nor 連接，那麼動詞使用單數或複數，則視哪一個主詞與動詞較為接近。

Example:

1. Either the bookshelves or the desk **have** to be moved out of the office. ····· (✕)
2. Either the bookshelves or the desk **has** to be moved out of the office. ······· (〇)

在這個例子中，the desk 較接近動詞，而這個主詞是單數，因此使用單數形動詞。

Exercise: 依照上一課所提到的原則，仿照第一題的方式，將題目中錯誤的地方畫底線，並重新寫出正確的句子。

1. Neither the Asian students nor the professor <u>were</u> wrong.

   Neither the Asian students nor the professor was wrong.

2. Working full-time and to take care of her children have taken up most of the mother's time.

   _____

3. Is you or Sam the president of the student council?

   _____

4. What the school needs is not money but build the trust between teachers and students.

   _____

5. Either the owner or the security guards has the key to the apartment.

   _____

6. Rick loves not only going to the movies but also to play online games.

   _____

7. Both teaching classes and to research are Dr. Jorgenson's responsibilities as a professor.

   _____

8. Neither Mr. Davidson's sons nor his daughter want to live with him.

   _____

Listen for Real

Whatever language you speak, listening is a very important cross-cultural skill. However, it takes practice to learn well. To be a good listener, one has to learn several listening skills: providing nonverbal [1]**feedback**, avoiding [2]**defensive** behaviors, [3]**evaluating** messages, and showing [4]**empathy**.

5   Good listeners give active nonverbal feedback to speakers. In other words, they look at the speakers most of the time and indicate with their facial expressions and body language that they are listening. They often nod and smile to speakers and allow speakers to finish their words.

10   In addition, good listeners should know how to avoid defensive behaviors, especially when the speakers try "too hard" to [5]**persuade** the listeners. Defensive behaviors include suddenly crossing the arms or stepping farther away from the speaker. Instead, good listeners should give positive feedback to encourage the speakers to talk.

15   Good listening also involves evaluating messages. This requires the listener to first understand the message of the speaker and then evaluate the message with an open mind. Evaluating often involves asking questions to understand. For example, an American student and a Taiwanese student might be

20 [6]**discussing** religion in their countries, which are very different. It is important for both students to ask appropriate questions that indicate interest but not judgment.

    Good listeners also show empathy. This means putting oneself [7]**in others' shoes**, and trying to understand how the speakers might feel. In order

25 to do so, listeners must reach beyond the words of speakers and [8]**explore** their emotions. For example, listeners can try to [9]**paraphrase** the words of the speakers and reflect feelings expressed by the speakers.

    An estimated 6,912 languages are spoken in the world

30 today. No matter what language you speak, always remember that listening is a [10]**universal** art that can encourage cross-cultural understanding.

> *see Tips for Advanced Readings page 107*

An Eye for an Eye

An American [1]**professor** is becoming annoyed in one of her classes. When she tries to make eye contact with every member of the class, she notices that some of the Asian students are avoiding her eyes. She feels that they are hiding something from her. In reality, the Asian students are just showing respect for her position of [2]**authority**.

Making eye contact has different meanings in different cultures. Looking into a person's eyes may make him or her

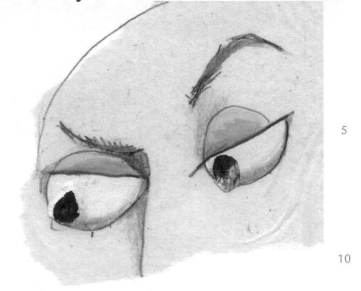

5

10

uncomfortable, or it can create a sense of [3]**connection**. It all depends on where the person is from. The Westerners tend to make frequent, longer-lasting eye contact than those from Eastern cultures. So, when talking to people from other cultures, it is important to know 15 what eye contact means to them.

For example, the [4]**Native Americans** have their special view of eye contact. They believe that direct, lasting eye contact could steal a person's soul. So, when you talk to a Native American next 20 time, be careful not to look at him or her directly in the eye.

In Japan, a professor may be upset when American students give him or her longer-lasting eye contact. To the professor, it could be misunderstood 25 as a challenge to her authority. The Japanese are not particularly comfortable with direct eye contact, and will sometimes look at the speaker's neck rather than into the person's eyes. It is rude in many Asian cultures to make eye contact with those in higher positions, or with [5]**the elderly**. 30

In some cultures, long-lasting eye contact can cause discomfort, or raise concerns about your [6]**intentions** toward a person. However, in American and European cultures, avoiding someone's eyes is a sign of dishonesty. Therefore, when speaking with someone of a different culture, try to make him or her comfortable with appropriate eye contact.

see Tips for Advanced Readings page 107

How would you like your bread?

❶ deep fry 炸	❹ stir fry 炒	❼ steam 蒸
❷ toast 烤 (吐司等)	❺ bake 烘焙	❽ barbecue 烤肉
❸ boil 煮	❻ stew 燉	❾ roast 烤 (用烤爐)

120 min

Ordering Food

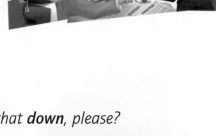

Henry (H) and Laura (L) are at a local restaurant. A waitress (W) is taking their order.

W: Hi. My name is Karen. I'm your waitress today. Are you ready to order now? Or you need a few more minutes?

H: I think we're ready. We'd like to have some ¹**tofu** with ²**century eggs** for ³**appetizer**. Oh, and some ⁴**kimchi**, too.

L: Century eggs? Are you sure about that?

H: Of course. You should try them. They are not as terrible as you think, dear.

L: Fine. I'll just give them a try.

H: Hey, they have Mapo tofu here! Let's have some of that!

L: That sounds better. (turning to the waitress) Can you ⁵**put** that **down**, please?

W: Sure. Anything else?

L: Umm.... ⁶**Beef with green pepper** sounds good.

H: Sure. We'd like to have that as well. And have we ordered anything to drink?

L: No, I don't think so. How about some hot tea, Henry?

H: Just what I was thinking!

W: So, that's hot tea for the drink.

L: That's right. And I think that will be all for now.

Tips for You

1. (Mapo) tofu *n.* (麻婆) 豆腐
2. century egg 皮蛋
3. appetizer [`æpə‚taɪzɚ] *n.* 開胃菜
4. kimchi [`kɪmtʃɪ] *n.* 泡菜
5. put...down 寫下
6. beef with green pepper 青椒牛肉

Listening Practice

(35) *First, take a few seconds to study the menu below. Then listen to the conversation and check (✓) what Chris orders from the menu. Don't forget the extra notes on his order.*

GOURMET HOUSE JOE'S

Menu

APPETIZERS

- ☐ Onion Rings
- ☐ Buffalo Wings
- ☐ Fried Calamari
- ☐ Chicken Strips

SANDWICHES & BURGERS

- ☐ Ham & Cheese Sandwich
- ☐ Chicken Sandwich
- ☐ Cheeseburger
- ☐ BLT (Bacon, Lettuce, & Tomato)
- ☐ Hamburger
- ☐ Veggie Burger

PASTAS

- ☐ Garlic Shrimp Pasta
- ☐ Meatball Spaghetti
- ☐ Lasagna

STEAK, SEAFOOD, & GRILL

- ☐ Rib Eye Steak
- ☐ T-Bone Steak
- ☐ Seafood Platter
- ☐ Grilled Chicken Breast
- ☐ Lamb Chops

BEVERAGES

Tea, Coffee, & Soft Drinks

- ☐ Hot Tea (Earl Grey or Fresh Mint)
- ☐ Iced Tea
- ☐ Cappuccino
- ☐ Espresso
- ☐ Flavored Sodas (Cherry or Vanilla)
- ☐ Orange Juice
- ☐ Lemonade

Cocktails

- ☐ Long Island Iced Tea
- ☐ Cosmopolitan
- ☐ Sea Breeze
- ☐ Vanilla Sky

DESSERTS

- ☐ Banana Split Sundae
- ☐ Chocolate Velvet Tart
- ☐ Tiramisu
- ☐ Cheese Cake

Extra Notes:
_____
_____
_____

🎧 (36) Complaining About Food

1. *Excuse me! I think the fish has* ¹**gone bad/ spoiled***!*

4. *Sorry to bother you, but would you please send the* ⁵**spaghetti** *back to the kitchen? It's cold.*

2. *I'm afraid the steak is too* ²**raw***. Are you sure it's* ³**well-done***?*

5. *Excuse me! There is a hair/fly in my soup.*

3. *I think you've sent the* ⁴**egg drop soup** *to the wrong table. I don't remember ordering it.*

6. *I wonder when you'll bring me the extra* ⁶**syrup** *that I ordered for my pancakes.*

Tips for You

1. go bad = spoil （食物）腐敗
2. raw [rɔ] *adj.* 生的，未煮熟的
3. well-done [ˋwɛlˋdʌn] *adj.* 全熟的
4. egg drop soup 蛋花湯
5. spaghetti [spəˋgɛtɪ] *n.* 義大利麵；義大利麵條
6. syrup [ˋsɪrəp] *n.* 糖漿

Oral Practice

Work in pairs and complete the following dialogues. Take turns playing the roles of a customer (C) and a waiter/waitress (W). Use the expressions on the previous page wherever appropriate.

W: What can I do for you?

C : _____

_____

W: Sure. And I'll make sure your steak will come out just the way you like it—well-done and juicy.

C : Thank you.

W: Is everything OK here?

C : _____

_____

W: Oh, I'm terribly sorry about that. I'll come back with a fresh bowl of soup.

C : I don't think I'd like that. Let me speak with your manager.

W: Is there anything I can do for you?

C : _____

_____

W: Oh, the coke! Sorry about that. It'll be right on your table in a minute.

C : I'd really appreciate it.

W: Is everything fine here?

C : _____

_____

W: Oh, I'm sorry. Let me check who ordered the spaghetti.

C : Thank you. And, would you please take it away first?

 **All About the Taste?**

Believe it or not, differences in ¹**dietary** choices sometimes ²**have very little to do with** how the food tastes. They have more to do with cultural differences.

For example, to the South Koreans, dog meat can be made into a ³**delicacy**. 5 However, to the Americans, it is difficult to imagine themselves eating anything made of dog meat. This has nothing to do with how the food tastes, but with what "dogs" are viewed as in the two cultures.

In certain parts of South Korea, dogs are like chickens. They are raised as farm animals and regarded as ⁴**sources** of food. On the other hand, to those 10 who grew up in the American culture, dogs are pets and should never be served on the dinner table.

In addition, while steaks are common in the American diet, they are often absent from the traditional Indian diet. This is because most Indians are ⁵**Hindus**, to whom ⁶**cattle**—especially ⁷**cows**—are ⁸**sacred** and must not be served as 15 food. However, in the U.S., where cattle are raised for food, there is no reason not to eat them.

⁹**By the same token**, the reason why ¹⁰**Muslims** don't eat pork has nothing to do with how it tastes. It has a lot to do with the fact that pigs are "unclean" according to Muslim teachings.

Tips for You

1. dietary [`daɪə͵tɛrɪ] *adj.* 飲食的
   diet [`daɪət] *n.* 飲食
2. have little/much to do with...
   與⋯不甚 / 非常相關
3. delicacy [`dɛləkəsɪ] *n.* 佳餚
4. source [sors] *n.* 來源
5. Hindu [`hɪndu] *n.* 印度教徒
   Hinduism [`hɪndu͵ɪzəm] *n.* 印度教

6. cattle [`kætl̩] *n.* (*pl.*) 牛 (總稱)
7. cow [kaʊ] *n.* 母牛
8. sacred [`sekrɪd] *adj.* 神聖的
9. by the same token   同樣地
10. Muslim [`mʌzləm] *n.* 回教徒，穆斯林
    Muslim [`mʌzləm] *adj.* 回教的

I. *Based on the reading, match the items on the right with those on the left.*

1. In the U.S., ...

2. To Muslims, ...

3. In South Korea, ...

4. To Hindus, ...

...pigs are considered "unclean."

...dogs are raised as farm animals.

...cows are sacred animals.

...dogs are mostly pets, not farm animals.

II. *Fill in each of the blanks with the correct answer.*

( ) 1. The fact that steaks are not part of the traditional Indian diet has much to
do with _____.
(A) Hinduism   (B) Muslim teachings
(C) their taste   (D) none of the above

( ) 2. According to the reading, pork is not part of the traditional _____
diet.
(A) Hindu   (B) South Korean
(C) American   (D) Muslim

( ) 3. Whether dogs can be killed for food has much to do with _____.
(A) what they are fed with
(B) how much their meat costs
(C) what they are viewed as in a culture
(D) how delicious their meat tastes

Avoid Irrelevance

寫作時，所有的句子都必須與段落的主題句 (topic sentence) 環環相扣，才能使段落不偏離主題。因此，文章裡每個句子都必須以主題句一一檢視。任何與主題句不相關的句子，都算是不對題 (irrelevance)，因此必須予以刪除或修改。

Exercise: 選出與主題句不相關的句子。

(　　) 1. Topic Sentence: Some foods are served only on special days.

    (A) On New Year's Day, the Greeks eat a special type of bread with a coin inside.

    (B) In Japan, it is important to have lobster when celebrating a person's birthday.

    (C) Stinky tofu is a popular dish that is commonly seen in Taiwan's night markets.

(　　) 2. Topic Sentence: Having too much fast food could result in health problems.

    (A) Most doctors have advised people against fast food.

    (B) The number of fast-food restaurants is growing.

    (C) Some heart diseases have something to do with fast food.

(　　) 3. Topic Sentence: Rice is commonly seen in most Asian diets.

    (A) Steamed rice is essential to a traditional Chinese or Japanese meal.

    (B) It is uncommon for a Taiwanese restaurant not to serve rice.

    (C) Fried rice is becoming a popular dish in some American restaurants.

Avoid Shifts in Person

同一段或是同一篇文字裡，使用的人稱 (person) 應當避免更動，方可使全篇或全段具有整體感及一致性。例如：如果使用第二人稱的 you 開始撰文，就不適宜在段落中途轉換成第一人稱的 I 或 we。

Exercise: 在以下各題文字中，找出「人稱更動」的句子，並在其下畫底線。

1. The South Korean are said to raise dogs as farm animals and kill them for food. If you grew up in certain areas of Asia, you probably have heard about the idea of "eating dogs." However, in the American culture, people usually keep dogs as pets, and they will never serve dogs' meat on their plates.

2. For most of us, eating insects seems like a scary idea. What we usually do is kill or stay away from those creatures. However, in northern Thailand, you cannot get a taste for the local food culture without trying the snacks made of insects.

3. In ancient Italy, people baked plain bread and covered it in oil, olives, or small fish. Later, they started putting other types of meat and vegetables on the bread before they baked it. Eventually, what we call "pizza" today came into being.

Advanced Reading I

Bugs for Breakfast

While eating insects is a [1]**taboo** in the West, it has been part of various food cultures for thousands of years. Believe it or not, more than 1,200 kinds of insects have been considered "food."

palm weevil

5　　　The [2]**Nigerians** are among the world's best-known insect eaters. They roast [3]**termites** over a fire or fry them in a pot. [4]**Grasshoppers** and [5]**crickets**, with their insides taken out, are also roasted. The juicy [6]**larvae** of [7]**palm weevils** are
10　fried and made into a Nigerian delicacy. High in fat, these larvae are said to taste like [8]**taros**.

Other than the Nigerians, the Japanese also boil [9]**wasp** larvae and fry grasshoppers. In [10]**Bali**, [11]**dragonflies** are barbecued or boiled with ginger,
15　garlic, and coconut milk before they are served on the dinner table. For those who live in northern Thailand, fried [12]**scorpions** are among their favorite snacks.

dragonfly

Although eating insects is understandably a
20　taboo in Western cultures, there is no scientific basis for it. In fact, most insects are safe to eat, especially when they are fully cooked. Some of them are excellent sources of [13]**protein**. When dealing with insects that are [14]**poisonous**, people have learned how to cook them without getting poisoned.

25　　　So, really, why is the idea of "bugs for breakfast" so scary in one culture but acceptable in another? It is safe to say that the answer is more about cultural differences than science.

see Tips for Advanced Readings page 108

Advanced Reading II

What Not to Eat in India

As a huge country, India is home to more than one [1]**billion** people. However, not all Indians follow the same customs and share the same diet. Though living in the same country, the members of India's major religions have their individual food-related taboos.

Unlike most Westerners, Hindu Indians do not eat hamburgers or anything made of beef. It is because [2]**Krishna**, an important Hindu god, was said to have been a [3]**cowherd**. Since Krishna loved and protected cattle, especially cows, Hindus expect themselves to do the same. That's why a lot of cows and [4]**bulls** walk freely on India's streets instead of being raised and killed for food.

In addition to Hindus, Muslims make up another major religious group in India. They follow the teachings of the [5]**Koran**, which says that pigs are unclean. No one is quite sure 15 why the Koran says so, but it leads Muslims to believe that whoever eats pork will become unclean also. Eating pork, as a result, becomes one of the major dietary taboos among Muslim Indians.

Another religious group in India with its own dietary taboos [6]**consists of** [7]**Jains**. These people believe in peace and love for all living things, and so they do not eat anything that involves [8]**cruelty** to animals. Their diet, of course, does not include meat, fish, milk, cheese, honey, or eggs. Some of them believe that a plant is cruelly destroyed when its [9]**root** is taken away. Those Jains who believe so refuse to eat root vegetables, and most of their diet consists of fruits that fall from trees.

Once visitors to India learn about these dietary taboos in India's major religions, it will be easier for them to find out what 30 NOT to expect when they sit down at the dinner table with local Indians.

▶ see Tips for Advanced Readings page 108

I'd like to ask that tall, slender girl out.

❶ straight hair	直髮
❷ chubby	微胖的
❸ dark-skinned/ fair-skinned	皮膚黑 / 皮膚白的
❹ stocky	矮壯的
❺ crew cut	平頭
❻ paper-thin	(口語) 紙片般薄的
❼ pony tail	馬尾
❽ slender	纖細的，苗條的
❾ gray hair	灰白頭髮
❿ blond/blonde	金髮的 (女性 / 男性)
⓫ clean-cut	外表乾淨好看的 (指男性)
⓬ curly hair	卷髮
⓭ flat nose	塌鼻
⓮ bushy eyebrow	濃眉
⓯ fat/thin lips	厚 / 薄唇

Conversation & Useful Expressions I

🎧⁴² Describing Physical Appearance

1. *Laura (L) is having a dinner party at home with some colleagues from work. Chris (C) is asking her who has come to the party.*

C: *Mom, you said the* ¹ **CFO** *is here. Where is he?*

L: *Look over there. He's sitting on the couch—the stocky guy with curly hair.*

C: *Oh, that's him. And the lady sitting right next to him?*

L: *That's our manager at* ² **Human Resources**, *Ms. Jiang.*

C: *Oh, I've seen her in your office once. She wasn't so...chubby back then.*

L: *Chubby? She's three months'* ³ **pregnant**. *How rude of you, Chris!*

C: *Well, you should have told me that, Mom.*

2. *Chris (C) and Natalie (N) are on the way to a class. A girl walks past them.*

C: *Did you see that tall, slender girl?*

N: *She's in my Freshman English class.*

C: *Really? That's perfect!*

N: *What? You wanna ask her out?*

C: *That's exactly what I am thinking.*

N: *OK. Tell me what you like about her.*

C: *Everything. Her long, wavy hair. Her fat lips. Her slender* ⁴ **figure**. *Oh, and....*

N: *Chris, I hate to say this, but she'll never go out with you.*

C: *Why? Did I say anything wrong?*

N: *No. She is just NOT into* ⁵ **shallow** *guys like you.*

Tips for You

1. CFO *n.* (= Chief Financial Officer) 財務長
2. human resources 人事部門
3. pregnant [`prɛgnənt] *adj.* 懷孕的
4. figure [`fɪgjɚ] *n.* 身材
5. shallow [`ʃælo] *adj.* 膚淺的

Listening Practice

Listen to the conversations, and choose the correct answers.

_____ 1. The woman's co-worker _____.

(A) wears a red T-shirt

(B) comes up and says hi

(C) is tall and chubby

(D) works with Michael

_____ 2. The woman has _____.

(A) long, gray hair

(B) a son with gray hair

(C) a 14-year-old son

(D) short, curly hair

_____ 3. The man _____.

(A) has blond hair

(B) doesn't like a crew cut

(C) thought his hair was too short

(D) said he liked his long, blond hair

_____ 4. The woman likes _____.

(A) the stocky guy with fair skin

(B) the stocky guy with dark skin

(C) the slender guy with fair skin

(D) the slender guy with dark skin

_____ 5. The man _____.

(A) has a flat nose

(B) is the woman's husband

(C) thinks his wife is ugly

(D) is not married

_____ 6. The man _____ when the picture was taken.

(A) was thirty years old with fair skin

(B) was thirty years old with dark skin

(C) was on the school's basketball team

(D) was on the school's baseball team

Extending and Rejecting Invitations

1. Chris (C) ¹***runs into*** *Kelly (K) on the way out of the campus. He is asking her out on a date.*

C: *Hey, Kelly, what do you plan to do this weekend?*

K: *I don't have any plans for the weekend yet. Why?*

C: *I wonder if you'd be interested in going to a movie with me.*

K: *That sounds great. I'd love to.*

C: *Really? I'll check the movie schedules then. Can I call you later about this?*

K: *Sure. But now, I have to catch the bus.*

C: *Before you leave, let me get your cellphone number first.*

K: *Sure. It's 0900-555-193. Got it?*

C: *Got it. I'll call you tomorrow.*

K: *OK. Call me in the morning. Bye!*

2. Laura (L) is leaving her office for lunch. She is asking one of her assitants, Brandon (B), if he'd like to come along.

L: *Hey, Brandon, Ms. Jiang and I are going out for lunch. Wanna* ²***tag along****?*

B: *I'd love to, but I can't. I am waiting for a phone call.*

L: *Oh, come on.* ³***My treat****.* ⁴***What do you say?***

B: *Why don't you two go first, and let me call you on your cellphone later?*

L: *That'd work, too. When you call, I'll tell you where we're having lunch.*

B: *And I'll be there as soon as possible. Wait. You're not going to the dirty noodle shop we went to last time, are you?*

L: *No. We're going somewhere else today.*

B: *Good. I'll call you in fifteen minutes or so. See you later!*

L: *See you later, Brandon.*

Tips for You

1. run into　偶遇

2. tag along　跟著 (某人) 去，參一腳

3. My treat.　我請客。

4. What do you say?　你覺得如何？

Work in pairs and complete each of the dialogues.

1

A: _____

B: Sunday night? No, actually, I'll be free all day. Why?

A: Would you be interested in going out for dinner with me?

B: Of course, _____ .

A: That's great. When is the best time to pick you up?

B: I think 6:30 will be a good time.

2

A: Are you joining me for the movie?

B: _____ , but I didn't bring my wallet with me.

A: I'll pay first. Just give me the money later. _____ _____

B: In that case, sure. Why not?

3

A: So, you are coming to my party on Saturday night, right?

B: I'm sorry, _____ . So, don't [1] **count me in**.

A: Babysit your sister? Can't you work something out?

B: I'll try, but I can't promise anything.

A: When are you going to know for sure?

B: Tomorrow, I think.

A: I'd really like to see you in the party. _____ _____

B: Sure. Call me in the afternoon.

Tips for You

1. count...in 把…算進去，算…一份

Happy Meal or ¹Rumbling Stomach?

To many of us, it is difficult to decide what to say when we are offered food in a different culture. Is "Yes" the right answer, or "No"? Well, if you want to walk away politely from the dinner table with a full stomach, you need to consider the culture you are in before you ²**respond**.

5   Basically, there are two types of cultures: direct and indirect. Many Asian cultures are indirect cultures. That is, Asians usually don't verbally say "No" for a ³**negative** answer or reply. Instead, they say it with actions or nonverbal ⁴**cues**. However, in North America, people tend to say what they mean. That is, they say "Yes" for yes, and "No" for no.

In other words, when our ⁵**host** in a direct culture asks us, "Would you like to have
10 more salad?" We should respond by saying what we really want. The host will respect and believe what we say. "Yes" will bring us more food, while "No" will get us nothing. However, if we are in an indirect culture, we need to reply with "No, thank you very much," for the first time, because the host will surely ask again by saying, "Oh, but you must have more." After such a polite offer comes up more than once, we can then safely say "Yes"
15 without being considered rude.

In our first year of learning English, most of us were taught what "Yes" and "No" mean. But few of us know how complicated "Yes" and "No" can be in real life when we meet people from other cultures. A proper "Yes" or "No" would make each of us a very polite guest, who gets to have a happy meal at the dinner table.

Tips for You

1. rumbling [`rʌmblɪŋ] *adj.* 發出咕嚕聲的
   rumble [`rʌmbl̩] *v.* (肚子) 發出咕嚕聲
2. respond [rɪ`spɑnd] *v.* 回應
   response [rɪ`spɑns] *n.* 回應
3. negative [`nɛgətɪv] *adj.* 否定的；負面的
   positive [`pɑzətɪv] *adj.* 肯定的；正面的
4. cue [kju] *n.* 暗示，提示
5. host [host] *n.* (宴會、活動等的) 主人或主持人

I. *Choose the correct answers based on the reading.*

(   ) 1. What is the main idea of the reading?

      (A) Direct cultures are better for Americans.

      (B) Asians should learn how to say "No" directly and verbally.

      (C) Indirect cultures are better for building business relationships.

      (D) The way to say "Yes" and "No" varies from culture to culture.

(   ) 2. Usually, Asians give negative answers with _____ or _____.

      (A) actions; verbal expressions

      (B) actions; nonverbal cues

      (C) nonverbal cues; written expressions

      (D) nonverbal cues; verbal expressions

(   ) 3. Which of the following statements is true?

      (A) In indirect cultures, dinner hosts and hostesses believe that guests say what they really mean.

      (B) Asians usually say "Yes" for yes, and "No" for no.

      (C) The Americans would take a "Yes" from their guest as yes, and a "No" as no.

      (D) American culture is considered an indirect culture.

II. *Check (✓) the ideas that are included in the reading.*

☐ 1. American culture is a direct culture.

☐ 2. Most Asian cultures are indirect cultures.

☐ 3. Asians and Americans prefer different conversation topics at the dinner table.

☐ 4. Compared with Asians, Americans are better at using nonverbal cues.

☐ 5. It is important to learn the differences between direct and indirect cultures.

Review: Avoid Irrelevance

完成段落的寫作後，還有幾個重要的步驟需要執行：

1. 檢查段落是否有主題句 (topic sentence)。如果有，它在段落裡位置是否恰當？通常，主題句應該是在段落的開頭幾句。

2. 找到主題句後，檢視段落中的各個句子，看看是否都與主題句相扣。

Exercise: 在下列段落中，找出主題句 (topic sentence) 以及不對題的句子 (irrelevant sentence)，並將號碼寫在下方空白欄。

❶The idea of "beauty" changes with time and culture. ❷If you lived in Japan in the 1800s and had sparkling white teeth, it would be difficult for you to find a wife or husband. ❸We are lucky to have dentists today. ❹Unlike today, black teeth were considered attractive by the Japanese in the 1800s. ❺In ancient Egypt, you would need a huge belly in order to be considered rich. ❻This is still true in some cultures today. ❼To be rich was considered attractive by Egyptians back then. ❽In the Middle Ages, the Europeans preferred fair skin because it meant "wealth" to them. ❾The rich were mostly fair-skinned because they would cover their bodies completely whenever they went outdoors. ❿Only poor people were dark-skinned because they had to work under the sun all day long.

topic sentence: _____

irrelevant sentence(s): _____

Review: Avoid Shifts in Person

為了避免段落中有人稱上的更動 (shift in person)，在完成寫作後，切記將整段文字從頭到尾重新檢視一次。

Exercise: 在以下段落中的空格內，填入適當的人稱。如空格內不需任何人稱，則以 × 替代。

    In today's business world, meetings and social events often take place during meals. It is important to understand the basic table manners in the West if your job requires lots of dinner appointments with Westerners.

    After sitting in the restaurant, you will see a napkin set on the table and you need to know how to use it. When the last guest sits, place the napkin on your lap, with the fold toward ❶_____ waist. If ❷_____ have to leave the table, excuse yourself to the host and place the napkin on the chair or to the left of ❸_____ plate. When you finish eating, the napkin goes to the right of your plate.

    When you eat, ❹_____ should learn eating manners as follows: wait until everyone has food, chew with mouth closed, and don't talk with food in ❺_____ mouth. Bring food to ❻_____ mouth, and avoid applying makeup, cleaning ❼_____ nails, or using a toothpick at the table. In addition, when someone needs items, pass the items to the right.

    If you learn table manners in another culture, ❽_____ will be able to show ❾_____ respect for that culture while ❿_____ eating with the people who live in it. Besides, showing good table manners will help ⓫_____ in business and social settings.

International Dining—Do Your Research!

If you are invited to a dinner in a foreign country, it is important to be informed about the culture's dining etiquette. Many [1]issues [2]come into play during international meals, such as seating, conversation topics, and gift-giving.

5 North Americans tend to be quite relaxed about seating arrangements, and guests often choose their own seats at the table. In Europe, however, guests should usually wait to sit down because there may be a seating plan. In France, for example, a "man-woman-man-woman" [3]alternation is respected, a custom 10 that dates back to the Middle Ages. But in some Middle Eastern countries, where relationships between men and women are distant, males and females will eat in separate rooms, or even in totally different locations.

Acceptable meal conversation topics also vary from culture to 15 culture. Americans don't hesitate to ask questions like "What do you do for a living?" or "Do you have children?" Although politics and religion are usually avoided, some Americans are very [4]outspoken about them, but they generally won't ask for your opinion. As to the French, they have great respect for privacy and 20 they are very careful about asking people questions. Unlike Americans, they would never ask someone they've just met questions about jobs, money, politics, or religions.

Gift giving at dinner table, in addition, can be complicated. Depending on the culture, certain objects must not be offered as 25 gifts. For instance, France and [5]Switzerland are famous for making high-[6]quality knives, and it is common to offer knives as gifts. However, the Chinese associate objects that "cut" things with "cutting off relationships," so never give them knives—not even letter openers—as gifts.

30 The subject of dining etiquette is so vast that perhaps there is only one solid piece of advice: do some research on the Internet first! You will learn a lot and avoid embarrassing your host—or yourself.

▶ see Tips for Advanced Readings page 108

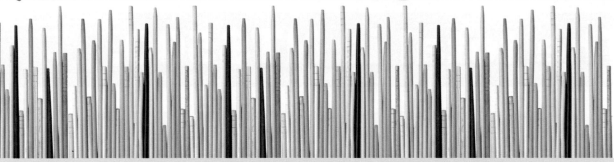

Knives, Forks, and Chopsticks

Every day, people all around the world sit down at the dinner table, but not everyone eats in the same way. Chopsticks, knives, forks, and even hands are all possible eating ¹**utensils**, depending on the culture the users live in.

Most Asians prefer to use chopsticks. It is believed this preference results from the living conditions in ancient times, and the cultural beliefs that are common in Asian cultures. 5 In ancient times, ²**fuel** was rare, and ³**chopping** food into bite-size pieces made it easier to cook food faster. This way of cooking helped save fuel. Also, in ancient Asia, meat was rarely available to ⁴**peasants**, so chopping it before cooking meant everyone could take a piece.

In most Western cultures, people eat with knives and forks. Fuel and meat weren't rare 10 in Europe in ancient times, so meat was usually roasted in large pieces. ⁵**Metal** was very expensive though, so in ancient Europe, diners brought their own forks and knives to cut meat. This also gave diners the ⁶**advantage** of having sharp ⁷**weapons** with them if a friendly meal turned into a bloody fight!

In most of India and the Middle East, people use their hands to pick up food. This can 15 be the most ⁸**sensible** of all choices—no special utensils are required, so there is no need to wash them! Also, in the Middle East, people believe that part of tasting the food is to feel it with their hands. Of course, only the right hand, which is always kept clean, is used to pick up food because the left hand is used for tasks like cleaning oneself. 20

What makes travel fun is not only the different tastes of food, but also the different ways of eating. Learning what to eat with, such as the correct hand—or knives, forks, and chopsticks—is an essential part in experiencing another culture. Next time you travel to a different country, be sure to give yourself a whole new experience with the local food by 25 "doing as the Romans do."

> see Tips for Advanced Readings
page 108

The total is NT$500.

❶ duty-free 免稅的

❷ try on 試穿，試戴

❸ discount 折扣

❹ cash 現金

❺ total 總價

❻ cashier 收銀員

❼ cash register 收銀機

❽ credit card 信用卡

❾ signature 簽名

❿ change 零錢

⓫ receipt 收據

⓬ coupon 折價券

⓭ gift certificate 禮券

⓮ trial period 試用期

⓯ warranty 保證書

⓰ refund 退貨

⓱ exchange 換貨

⓲ tax included 已含稅

🎧(50) Making Purchases

Chris (C) is shopping for a new pair of sneakers. A sales clerk (S) is helping him.

C: Hi. I'd like to.... Wait. Do you speak English?

S: Yes. What can I do for you?

C: Yes. I am looking for a pair of sneakers.

S: Are you looking for a particular brand?

C: Nope—as long as they are ¹**sturdy** enough.

S: These are our ²**new arrivals**. Would you like to try them on?

C: That will be great.

S: What size do you wear?

C: I wear size 10.

S: Here. These are size 10.

C: Let me try them on.
   (a few seconds later)

C: Hey, they fit—perfectly.

S: And, the color and style are
   right for you.

C: I'll take these—and a pair of the sports socks here.

S: The total is NT$2,500. Are you paying in cash or...?

C: I'd like to pay with my credit card.
   (a few seconds later)

S: OK. Mr. Parker. Please sign here.

C: *(putting down his signature on the* ³**slip***)* OK, here you are.

S: Thanks. This is your copy. And here are your receipt and credit card.

Tips for You

1. sturdy [ˋstɝdɪ] *adj.* 耐用的

2. new arrival   (剛上市的) 新品

3. slip [slɪp] *n.* 紙條

Listening Practice

51 *Listen to the conversations, and choose the correct answers.*

_____ 1. (A) The product costs NT$5,000.
    (B) The woman is looking for a TV set.
    (C) The product costs NT$20,000.
    (D) The woman is looking for NT$25,000.

_____ 4. (A) The woman gives the man a 3 percent discount.
    (B) The man wants to pay cash.
    (C) The man wants to pay with his credit card.
    (D) The woman refuses to take the man's credit card.

_____ 2. (A) The man is paying in cash.
    (B) The man is buying a T-shirt.
    (C) The man is applying for a new credit card.
    (D) The man is buying a shirt.

_____ 5. (A) The black car is bigger.
    (B) The green car looks better.
    (C) The green car costs NT$500,000.
    (D) The black car costs NT$500,000.

_____ 3. (A) The man promises to give the woman a discount.
    (B) The washing machine costs NT$50,000.
    (C) The woman can give the man a discount.
    (D) The washing machine is 10 percent off NT$50,000.

_____ 6. (A) The blue dress is size 40.
    (B) The green dress is bigger than the blue dress.
    (C) The blue dress costs NT$1,600.
    (D) The green dress costs more than the blue one.

Returning or Exchanging Merchandise

A: This MP3 player doesn't work. I'd like to return it and get a refund.

B: I'm sorry. The warranty ¹**expired** a week ago. We can't refund the MP3 player.

A: This computer ²**died on** me yesterday. Would you please refund it?

B: I need to see your receipt and the warranty first.

A: This T-shirt has a ³**stain** on it. Can I exchange it?

B: Sure. You can exchange it for a new one.

A: I'd like to exchange the baseball cap for this one.

B: Sure, but you'll have to pay the ⁴**price difference**. It's more expensive.

Tips for You

1. expire [ɪk`spaɪr] *v.* 過期
2. die on somebody (*infml.*) 故障
3. stain [sten] *n.* 污漬，髒污
4. price difference   差價

Work in pairs and complete each of the dialogues.

A: _____

It doesn't work at all.

B: Sure, but _____

_____.

A: Here they are.... The receipt—and the warranty.

B: Let me check.... OK. We'll exchange this Wii for a new one.

❷

A: _____

The first three pages are missing!

B: _____

A: Yes, I have it with me. Here is the receipt.

B: OK. We'll refund the book right away.

A: _____

_____ It broke a few days ago.

B: _____

_____, please?

A: Yes. Here are the receipt and the warranty.

B: I'm sorry, we can't exchange the sports watch. The warranty expired two days ago.

A Gift from the Heart

Jane was from Taiwan, and John from America. It was Christmas Day, and Jane couldn't wait to open the gift her new boyfriend had given her.

"Go ahead. Open it." John encouraged with a warm smile. Hearing this, Jane eagerly opened the box, and her face lit up with

5 joy when she saw the pink [1]**wool** sweater. "Oh, John, it's beautiful!" she cried, holding up the sweater to admire it. As she did, a small slip of paper dropped to the ground. A strange look came over Jane's face. "What's this?" she asked, holding up the paper.

"It's the receipt, of course," answered John.

10 "What's it doing in here? Did you forget to take it out?"

"No. I put it in there so you'd have it." John explained.

Jane tried her best to hide her surprise and anger at her boyfriend's poor manners. "Maybe I was wrong about this guy," she thought to herself.

Actually, neither of John and Jane is wrong here; it's simply a case of cultural misunderstanding. Jane feels offended because she thinks her boyfriend is being rude. In Taiwanese culture, it is considered impolite to [2]**reveal** how much one pays for a gift.

John, on the other hand, doesn't feel he did anything wrong. After all, giving Jane the receipt was a thoughtful thing to do. If Jane didn't like the sweater, or it was the wrong size, she could return it to the store with the receipt. This is quite [3]**normal** in John's culture.

Because of the differences in their cultural backgrounds, John and Jane have different ways of giving gifts and expressing thoughtfulness. What we learn in our culture affects how we [4]**interpret** acts of thoughtfulness, such as giving gifts. When giving gifts,
25 you should make sure that the recipient understands your intentions.

Tips for You

1. wool [wʊl] *n.* 羊毛

2. reveal [rɪ`vil] *v.* 洩漏；顯示

3. normal [`nɔrml] *adj.* 正常的

4. interpret [ɪn`tɝprɪt] *v.* 將⋯理解為⋯；
翻譯 (尤指口譯)

I. *Based on the reading, match the items on the right with those on the left.*

...is an American.

Jane...

...thinks it is rude to reveal how much one pays for a gift.

...is a Taiwanese.

John...

...believes giving the receipt of a gift to the recipient is a thoughtful thing to do.

II. *Choose the correct answers.*

(   ) 1. What did Jane think when she saw the receipt?

(A) John had hidden it in the sweater.

(B) John did not know it was there.

(C) John had forgotten to take it out.

(D) John did not buy the gift for her.

(   ) 2. According to the reading, the receipt of a gift is usually _____.

(A) hidden from the recipient in American culture

(B) given to the recipient in American culture

(C) hidden from the recipient in both American and Taiwanese cultures

(D) given to the recipient in both American and Taiwanese cultures

(   ) 3. John gave Jane the receipt of the sweater because _____.

(A) Jane records every dollar John spends on her

(B) the sweater might be the wrong size for Jane

(C) Jane had always asked for the receipt

(D) he indirectly asked Jane to pay for it

Supporting Sentences

段落中的支持句 (supporting sentence) 必須與主題句 (topic sentence) 密切相關，並且多用來解釋、說明、或證明主題句的內容。

Exercise: 在每題的選項中，選擇可用來當作支持句的句子。(可複選)

1. (   ) Topic Sentence: The best timing for opening gifts varies in different parts of the world.
   (A) In some cultures, it is considered impolite and embarrassing to open gifts immediately.
   (B) In Japan, people prefer elaborate wrapping, and this sometimes makes it very difficult to open a gift.
   (C) Westerners like to open gifts right away—in front of the givers—to show how much they honor the gifts.
   (D) The Chinese prefer to open gifts in private.

2. (   ) Topic Sentence: There are many ways to make the best of "buy two get one free" offers in supermarkets or department stores.
   (A) When shopping with a friend or co-worker, take the offer, divide the cost, and find a way to share the "bonus" product.
   (B) Some stores offer "buy two get one free" deals only on special days, and they always raise the prices first.
   (C) If one of your friends needs the product, buy two and share the free one as a gift with the friend.
   (D) If you don't have enough money to buy two of the product, forget about the offer and buy what you really need.

3. (   ) Topic Sentence: When you ask for a refund, be sure to bring what the store will ask from you before processing your request.
   (A) Sometimes, if you really like the product, you can exchange the one you bought for a new one.
   (B) If you bought the product on credit, the store will always ask you to show them the payment slip, which should have your signature on it.
   (C) The most important thing is the receipt, which proves that you really paid for the product.
   (D) In some cases, you will be asked to present your I.D., so don't forget to put it in your wallet or purse before heading to the store.

Avoid Shifts in Tense

同一段或是同一篇文字裡，即使文法上沒有錯誤，句子使用的基本時式 (primary tenses) 應當盡量保持一致，以避免讀者在閱讀上的困難或是理解上的混淆。以下是三大基本時式，以及從中衍生而來的其他時式：

1. 現在式：簡單現在式，現在完成式 (have/has + 過去分詞)，現在進行式 (is/am/are +V-ing)
2. 過去式：簡單過去式，過去完成式 (had + 過去分詞)，過去進行式 (was/were +V-ing)
3. 未來式：單純未來式，未來完成式 (will have + 過去分詞)，未來進行式 (will be +V-ing)

Exercise: 在以下各題文字中，找出「基本時式」不同的句子，並在其下畫底線。(可複選)

1. Gift giving has always been an art. It requires careful consideration of the recipient's cultural background. If you visit a Hindu Indian, you would have to remember NOT to offer a gift that is made of leather. To the Japanese, gifts of lilies or lotus blossoms can be very offensive. To older Taiwanese, "clocks" were never acceptable as gifts because they are associated with death. Also, remember to avoid anything that sounds like or are associated with "four" because it sounds like "death" in both Taiwanese and Mandarin Chinese.

2. Most stores have their own ways of getting shoppers to buy more. For example, the items that everyone needs are spread out in different parts of the store. If milk is in aisle 4, shoppers would have to go to aisle 7 to get bread. Shoppers are "forced" to see—and often tempted to buy—lots of other products before they finally get what they want to buy. Sometimes, the stores put little items on the shelves right next to the checkouts. That was why people would see chewing gum, candy bars, and small toys before getting to the cash register.

3. When a shopper sees something that catches his or her eye, what the shopper does often tells how wise the person is. Some people spent the money right away because they think it would be the last opportunity to get it. Others wait for the sales because it can help them get the lowest price. However, the wisest shoppers always buy what they really need. Those who make unwise choices often ended up with things that they would have no use of.

David was an American student visiting his friend Kumar, a Hindu Indian. It was Kumar's birthday and David was very proud of the gift that he had chosen, a leather jacket like the ones worn by [3]**cowboys** in Texas. Unfortunately, when Kumar opened the present, he [4]**exclaimed**, "Holy cow! A leather jacket!" Not

5   knowing that the cow is sacred to Hindus, David had offended his friend.

[1]Holy Cow! A [2]Leather Jacket!

The story tells us that gift giving is not just about giving gifts. It requires cultural understandings and—some thought. For example, even though both India and Japan are Asian countries, their gift giving customs are very different from each other.

In India, gift giving is a sign of friendship. Since Indians usually try to [5]**reciprocate** what they receive, do not give expensive gifts. Otherwise, this may cause embarrassment when the recipient cannot afford to reciprocate the gift. Also, gifts should not be opened when they are received. Instead, they are opened in private. And, remember to wrap gifts in bright, lucky colors such as red, green, or yellow.

In Japan, on the other hand, if you wish to give a gift of flowers, do not offer white flowers, such as [6]**lilies** or [7]**lotus**

20 blossoms, because these are usually used in funerals. Numbers are also very important. Do not give a gift that consists of the number "four" or "nine" because these numbers are considered unlucky. However, tasty food or quality alcohol is usually appreciated in a Japanese home. It is best to present the gift at the end of your visit—with both hands in a polite manner.

25 Also, there are some "safety tips" for gift giving. A box of sweets is always welcome. A gift from your own country that represents your culture will be valued. And, always remember to offer the gift with your right hand, or both hands, but never with the left hand only.

30 So, while traveling around the world or welcoming visitors into your home, remember to put some thought into the gift you give and how you give it.

▶ *see Tips for Advanced Readings page 109*

Environmental Ideas for Gift Giving

Do you know each year we use tons of paper to wrap our gifts, and most of this goes directly into garbage cans? We only have one earth, so we need to protect it while giving gifts. To do this, we can give environmentally friendly gifts and use [1]**unconventional** wrappings.

Some wrappings can help us protect the environment, including the [5]brown paper from paper bags, [2]**aluminum foil**, pages from old books or magazines, or even pieces of [3]**fabric** or old clothes. These can all be used

again afterwards or [4]**recycled**. Or what about wrapping a present inside another present, such as a pair of [5]**earrings** inside a small teacup, or an old book inside a new T-shirt? You can also buy beautiful wrappings made from recycled paper or other recycled [6]**materials**. If you use [7]**strings**, wool, or ribbons to tie the presents up, the paper can be used again!

But what are you going to put inside the wrapping that is good for the planet? If the person you are buying the present for likes the outdoors,

you could give plants, [8]**seeds**, or a bird house for their garden. Or you [15]could [9]**adopt** a zoo animal or a part of a [10]**rain forest**. There are also gifts that help save energy, like [11]**solar chargers** for iPods.

If you haven't got very much money, you could make a gift of your time and help. Think of something you are good at, like babysitting, cleaning, gardening or making a cake. These gifts are extra-special, and [20] there won't be anything to throw away afterwards!

Also, you could make a donation to an environmental charity as a gift for someone. This helps the environment in two ways. First, these gifts produce no waste because they need no wrapping. Second, they help support projects that help save rain forests or protect birds, which are good for the planet.

We can all do things to protect the environment, and even small things like giving environmentally friendly gifts or using unconventional wrappings will make a difference. By doing so, we can show our family and friends how easy and fun it is, and perhaps encourage them to do the same!

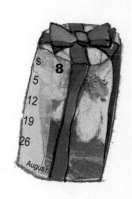

▶ *see Tips for Advanced Readings*
page 109

Sales Manager Wanted

JOBS-GENERAL

Publishing

SALES MANAGER

San Min Book Co., Ltd., a leading publisher in Taiwan, is looking for a SALES MANAGER.

Qualification:
- Excellent verbal communication skills
- High proficiency in Mandarin Chinese, Taiwanese, and English
- At least 3 years of experience in sales and marketing

Job Description:
- Finding potential customers
- Visiting and negotiating with current customers
- Managing and training 6-10 sales representatives

Type of Position:
This is a full-time, permanent position.

Location: Taipei

Salary: NT$40,000/Month

Benefits:
Company Car, Bonus, Labor Insurance, National Health Insurance, Free Meals

For immediate consideration, please send a Word or HTML version of your résumé to jobs@sanmin. com.tw.

Journalism

JOBS-G

Education
TEAC

Education

A
CO

Education

DRIVERS

❶ job/classified ad 徵才廣告	
❷ qualification(s)	資格
❸ job description	工作內容
❹ permanent/temporary position 常任 / 臨時的工作職位	
❺ salary	(責任制的) 薪水
❻ benefit(s)	員工福利
❼ company car	公司配給車
❽ résumé	履歷
❾ wage	工資 (指體力勞動者的 日薪或週薪)
❿ pay raise	加薪
⓫ overtime	加班時間；加班費
⓬ on-call	隨時待命的
⓭ entry-level	最基層的
⓮ expense account 開支帳戶	

58 Describing Personality Traits

Laura (L) is interviewing Johnny Wu (J), who applied for the position of her personal assistant.

L : How would you describe yourself as an employee?

J : I'm always self-motivated and easygoing at work. And, I always do my best to ¹*accomplish* what I'm asked to do.

L : It seems you are very ²**sure of yourself**. Now, Mr. Wu, tell me why I should hire you, not the other candidates?

J : Because I'm very ³**dependable**, detail-⁴**oriented**, and quick to find out what people need. I've also worked as an ⁵**administrative** assistant in the past.

L : Any of your strengths you'd like to add?

J : Yes. Working to deadlines has never been a problem for me, and I know how to ⁶**maintain** a high level of job performance under stress.

L : Great. Sounds like you have what I'm looking for in an assistant.

J : I'm very glad to hear that, Ms. Parker.

L : But, it'll be a few days before I make the final decision.

J : I understand. It always takes time to make the best decision.

L : All right, thanks for coming today, Mr. Wu.

J : Thank you, Ms. Parker, for the opportunity to speak with you.

L : We'll give you further notice in a few days.

Tips for You

1. accomplish [ə`kɑmplɪʃ] *v.* 達成

2. sure of oneself　有自信

3. dependable [dɪ`pɛndəbl] *adj.* 可靠的

4. oriented [`ɔrɪ,ɛntɪd] *adj.* 重視…；以…為取向

5. administrative [əd`mɪnə,stretɪv] *adj.* 行政的

6. maintain [men`ten] *v.* 保持，維持

Listening Practice

🎧 59 *Two hairstylists are talking about three clients. Listen to their conversations, and check (✓) the personality traits that they mention about each client.*

	Ms. Peterson 1.	Ms. Tennyson 2.	Ms. Flanner 3.
easygoing			
loud			
picky			
patient			
confident			
talkative			
shy			
humorous			

Conversation & Useful Expressions II

🎧⁶⁰ Expressing Preferences for People

Laura (L) and Brandon (B) are going over the job applications and talking about the applicants who came in to interview.

B: So, which one would you go for?

L: I'll tell you later. I'd like to know what you think about these people.

B: I think...Betty Chen will make a wonderful assistant.

L: Why? Don't tell me you have a crush on her.

B: No. I just prefer someone... ¹**sociable**...and ²**intelligent**. Look, she was Miss University before.

L: We're not looking for an intelligent " ³**social butterfly**," Brandon.

B: I know but....

L: ⁴**Tell you what**. I think Johnny Wu ⁵**stands out** as the best applicant.

B: Because...?

L: Because I'd like to have an assistant who is goal-oriented and responsible, rather than sociable and...beautiful.

B: Hey, I know you'd rather have an assistant like that. But I have to work with your new assistant, too.

L: Well, I have to think for myself first, Brandon.

B: All right, all right. ⁶**After all**, you're the boss.

Tips for You

1. sociable [ˈsoʃəbl] *adj.* 善於交際的
2. intelligent [ɪnˈtɛlədʒənt] *adj.* 聰明的
3. social butterfly　交際花

4. (I'll) tell you what.　我的想法是…
5. stand out　脫穎而出
6. after all　畢竟

Oral Practice

Work in pairs and complete each of the dialogues.

1. You and your housemate are looking for someone to share the apartment. Several people have come in and spoken with you. Now, you two are talking about who will make the best housemate.

> A: I think _____ because _____
>
> _____.
>
> B: I see. You prefer _____.
>
> A: Yeah. Don't you prefer a housemate like that, too?
>
> B: Not really. _____
>
> A: Quiet and friendly? But people like that are boring! I know _____
>
> _____ but I have to live with the new housemate, too!
>
> B: I know, but we already have someone who is too energetic and sociable...AND can't stop [1]**yapping**. And that person is YOU!

2. Tomorrow, you and your friend are going to vote for a new president of the [2]student council. Now you are talking about who you'll vote for.

> A: Both candidates are great, but _____.
>
> B: Really? So, _____ who is _____
>
> and _____.
>
> A: Yeah, don't you think it takes an intelligent president to lead the student council?
>
> B: That I understand, but good-looking? _____
>
> _____
>
> A: Creative and aggressive? I know _____ but people like that are usually [3]**egomaniacs**!
>
> B: [4]**Says who?**

Tips for You

1. yap [jæp] *v.* 喋喋不休地說話
2. student council 學生會
3. egomaniac [ˌigoˋmenɪˏæk] *n.* 自大狂
4. Says who? 誰說的？(表不贊同)

Short Reading

How to [1]Flunk an Interview

Your job interview at the Cash Bank is scheduled for tomorrow. Unfortunately, spending the summer working as a [2]**teller** at the bank is your father's idea. You'd rather be a lifeguard at the beach.

No problem. If you follow this simple advice about how to make an impression during your job interview, you can [3]**rest assured** that sunshine and [4]**surf** will be in your future.

First, make yourself comfortable when filling out the job application. Lie on the floor.

Second, don't bother to find out anything about the business of the bank or what a teller actually does. That way you can simply answer, "Not a single thing," when the interviewer asks, "What do you know about the job?"

Third, dress as though you're going to the beach: a [5]**Hawaiian** shirt, [6]**baggy** shorts, and [7]**flip-flops**. Sunglasses would be a nice touch, too.

Fourth, talk a lot so the interviewer can't ask too many questions. If the interviewer does manage to ask a question or two, give one-word answers, and at all times, avoid eye contact.

Fifth, if the interviewer asks about your last job, complain loudly about it. Mention that your last employer didn't like your attitude, and ask, "Is it a problem if I'm angry all the time?"

Finally, be prepared with a good answer for the trick question. A popular choice of interviewers is: "If you could be anyone in history, who would you be?" Unless you want to be a teller, forget about answering the question with "Mother Theresa." "Paris Hilton" would be a better choice. Answer with names like this, and you can count on the interview ending with the time-honored conclusion, "Don't call us. We'll call you." The translation of those words is: "Make other plans because you sure won't be working at the Cash Bank this summer."

Tips for You

1. flunk [flʌŋk] v. 沒通過 (考試等)
2. teller [ˋtɛlɚ] n. (銀行) 櫃員、出納員
3. rest assured　儘管放心
   assured [əˋʃʊrd] adj. 有保證的
   assure [əˋʃʊr] v. 保證；確保
4. surf [sɝf] n.; v. 海浪，浪花；衝浪

5. Hawaiian [həˋwaɪjən] adj.; n. 夏威夷 (人) 的；夏威夷人
   Hawaii [həˋwaɪjə] n. 夏威夷
6. baggy [ˋbægɪ] adj. 寬鬆的
7. flip-flop [ˋflɪp͵flɑp] n. 夾腳拖鞋

I. *Choose the correct answers based on the reading.*

(   ) 1. The person in the reading, who is referred to as "you," applies for a job to work as _____.
      (A) a lifeguard   (B) a sales representative
      (C) an interviewer   (D) a bank teller

(   ) 2. When asked about your last job, you should _____ in order to flunk an interview.
      (A) express gratitude for the company
      (B) complain about it
      (C) keep constant eye contact
      (D) share what you've learned from it

(   ) 3. Be sure to _____ if you want to flunk a job interview.
      (A) learn about the position
      (B) give well-thought-out answers
      (C) dress formally and appropriately
      (D) lie on the floor when filling out the job application

II. *Based on the reading, check (✓) the correct answers to the following question.*

To give the interviewer bad impressions, you should _____.
☐ 1. avoid wearing flip-flops or a Hawaiian shirt
☐ 2. wear baggy pants and give one-word answers
☐ 3. avoid eye contact at all times when the interviewer asks you questions
☐ 4. keep yourself from acting inappropriately, such as lying on the floor
☐ 5. talk a lot so that the interviewer can't ask you questions

Review: Supporting Sentences

段落的草稿完成後，務必以主題句 (topic sentence) 的內容，檢驗哪些句子適合留下來當作支持句 (supporting sentence)，這樣才能確保段落的內容與主題句相符，而不致顯得雜亂無章。

Exercise: 以下是一篇文章的草稿，畫底線的是主題句。從段落中找出適合當作支持句的句子，將對應的號碼填在下面的空白欄。

When you are in a job interview, there are some dos and don'ts that you should be aware of. ❶Don't send a letter of application without a well-written résumé. ❷Never interrupt your interviewer. ❸Wait until the interviewer finishes the question even if you already have an answer in mind. ❹In addition, when the company calls for an interview, it's OK to ask who is going to interview you and what position the person holds in the company. ❺And, choose the company you'd like to work for very carefully. ❻And, be confident, enthusiastic, and energetic. ❼Sending a letter of application without a résumé is a no-no. ❽Prepare the questions you'd like to ask the interviewr a couple days in advance. ❾If you can't talk about yourself confidently, it will be difficult to give the interviewer good impressions. ❿Arrive for the interview at least ten minutes early. ⓫Take a few seconds before you give the answer.

supporting sentence(s): _____

Writing II

Review: Avoid Shifts in Tense

同一段落的文字，時常會出現基本時式 (primary tense) 不相同的狀況。然而，為了不致造成文法上的錯誤，或是使讀者誤解句子的意思，寫作時仍應盡量選擇一個統一的基本時式。

Exercise: 以下是一篇幾乎完成的文章。首先，找出適合的主要時式；之後，在上述的前提下，將時式需要更改的句子號碼標於下面空白欄。

❶*Born to Rebel* is one of the first books to examine the connection between birth order and personality. ❷The author of the book was Frank Sulloway, a social historian. ❸Detailing the analysis of the lives of famous historical figures, the book contained interesting discoveries made by Sulloway.

❹One of the discoveries is that firstborn children usually do not cause problems for their parents. ❺Because they wanted to defend their special position in the family, they are often conservative and do not welcome change. ❻Although firstborns are born leaders, they are usually not risk takers. ❼Some famous firstborns included George W. Bush, Hillary Rodham Clinton, and Oprah Winfrey (歐普拉).

❽Another discovery is that later-born children are more likely to be rebels. ❾They are open to new experiences, and they are not afraid to try new things. ❿Many develop excellent communication and social skills. ⓫Some even become excellent performers and comedians, perhaps to get the attention of parents and older siblings. ⓬Copernicus (哥白尼), Charles Darwin, and Jim Carrey were some well-known later-born children.

⓭Although some critics claim that *Born to Rebel* does not contain anything new, millions of people have bought Sulloway's book. ⓮Thanks to Frank Sulloway and his book, the debate about whether birth order affects a person's personalities will continue on.

answer(s): _____

To [1]Veil or Not to Veil?

Both Europe and the U.S. have millions of [2]immigrants. In other words, for people who live in Europe and the U.S., it is possible for them to observe different living, eating, and religious customs. However, seeing or learning about these differences is not the same as accepting them.

5   In recent years, a large number of Muslims have immigrated to Europe. Most of them are very religious. To these people, following all the religious rules is an important part of their lives. For example, many Muslim women feel [3]obliged to wear a special veil, called a burka, wherever they go. Because the veil covers the entire face except for the eyes, some non-Muslims find this uncomfortable or unacceptable. This can give rise to difficulties in the
10   workplace when the employer feels that wearing a burka may [4]interfere with the quality of job performance. There is one case in Britain. A woman teaching assistant was fired from her job because she wore a burka at work. Some students complained that they could not hear her voice properly.

Interestingly, one Muslim woman in the [5]Netherlands, Samira Haddad, found that she
15   was denied employment for her refusal to wear a burka. Although she was a Muslim, she chose not to wear the traditional veil. When she was interviewed for a teaching position at the Islamic College in Amsterdam, she was told that she could not be offered a position because of her refusal to wear a burka. She sued the college and won the case because the court believed that she was [6]discriminated against.

20   To veil or not to veil is a personal choice. Americans, Europeans, or Asians should all remember that when observing any difference in clothing, understanding and even appreciation are much better than discrimination.

> see Tips for Advanced Readings page 109

Advanced Reading II

You Are What You Wear

In New York, a group of international executives gather for a meeting for the first time. The German arrives first, looking neat in his business suit. The Englishman shows up in his dark [1]**pinstriped** suit and white shirt. After a few minutes, their American boss, with his tie hanging loosely, walks in. The last to appear is the Italian, perfectly smart-looking in his Giorgio Armani suit and [2]**crisp** colored shirt.

5

Though all are wearing suits, the executives' clothes still say a lot about their cultural backgrounds. After all, clothing preferences and choices

10

are influenced by climate, human relations, and many other local factors. Take climate for example. Warm climates have tended to produce bright colors, like the [3]**saris** of India, while in Northern Europe, where the weather is cold, colors like dark blue and black help to keep the heat. Choosing the wrong color can sometimes result in embarrassing misunderstandings. In Europe, black is very [4]**chic** but in some countries, it is associated with

15

death and would not be worn to a happy occasion such as a wedding or company opening.

In terms of human relations, where [5]**group identity** is considered important and valued, uniforms are common. A Japanese manager might wear a factory [6]**overall** when he or she visits the production site to fit in with the workers. In the West, a CEO or general manager would still be in a suit.

20

Although there is no universal dress code for all business cultures in the world, most businesspeople tend to wear suits. But as the executives in our story show, there are tiny differences in how to choose and wear a suit. These differences may affect the first impression that people have about the wearer of the suit.

Towards the end of the meeting, the casual American takes off his jacket and [7]**rolls up** his [8]**sleeves**. "Let's get down to work," he says. The Europeans exchange looks and think to themselves, "How [9]**sloppy!**"

25

▶ see Tips for Advanced Readings page 109

Tips for Advanced Readings

Advanced Reading I (*page 20*)

1. etiquette [ˈɛtɪˌkɛt] *n.* 禮儀
2. value [ˈvælju] *v.* 重視
   valuable [ˈvæljəbl] *adj.* 有價值的
3. custom [ˈkʌstəm] *n.* 習俗
4. expert [ˈɛkspɚt] *n.* 專家
5. Ph.D.　博士學位
6. title [ˈtaɪtl] *n.* 頭銜
7. compare [kəmˈpɛr] *v.* 比較
8. strict [strɪkt] *adj.* 嚴格的
9. observe [əbˈzɝv] *v.* 遵守；觀察

Advanced Reading II (*page 21*)

1. challenge [ˈtʃælɪndʒ] *n.* 挑戰
2. partner [ˈpɑrtnɚ] *n.* 伙伴
3. cut and dried　事先安排好的
4. start out as　以⋯開始著手
5. rude [rud] *adj.* 無禮的
6. length [lɛŋθ] *n.* 長度
7. Latin American　拉丁美洲 (人) 的；拉丁美洲人
8. Arabic [ˈærəbɪk] *adj.* 阿拉伯 (人) 的
9. distance [ˈdɪstəns] *n.* 距離
10. wisdom [ˈwɪzdəm] *n.* 智慧
11. When in Rome, do as the Romans do
    入境隨俗
12. international [ˌɪntɚˈnæʃənl] *adj.* 國際的

Advanced Reading I (*page 32*)

1. walk on thin ice　如履薄冰
2. personally [ˈpɝsn̩lɪ] *adv.* 就個人而言
   personal [ˈpɝsn̩l] *adj.* 個人的
3. focus [ˈfokəs] *v.* 集中 (注意力等)
4. information [ˌɪnfɚˈmeʃən] *n.* 資訊
   inform [ɪnˈfɔrm] *v.* 告知
5. agreement [əˈgrimənt] *n.* 同意；一致
   agree [əˈgri] *v.* 同意；與⋯一致
6. involve [ɪnˈvɑlv] *v.* 涉入，參與
   involvement [ɪnˈvɑlvmənt] *n.* 牽涉，參與
7. gender [ˈdʒɛndɚ] *n.* 性別
8. insensitive [ɪnˈsɛnsətɪv] *adj.* 感覺遲鈍的；不敏感的
   sensitive [ˈsɛnsətɪv] *adj.* 有感覺的；敏感的
9. unproductive [ˌʌnprəˈdʌktɪv] *adj.* 無成效的
   productive [prəˈdʌktɪv] *adj.* 有成效的

Advanced Reading II (*page 33*)

1. workplace [ˈwɝkˌples] *n.* 職場，工作場所
2. Equal Rights Amendment　(the ~) 權利平等修正案
   amendment [əˈmɛndmənt] *n.* 修正案
3. constitution [ˌkɑnstəˈtjuʃən] *n.* 憲法
4. position [pəˈzɪʃən] *n.* 職位
5. political [pəˈlɪtɪkl] *adj.* 政治的
   politics [ˈpɑləˌtɪks] *n.* 政治
6. salary [ˈsælərɪ] *n.* 薪資
7. make up　組成
8. exist [ɪgˈzɪst] *v.* 存在
9. aggressive [əˈgrɛsɪv] *adj.* 好勝的；具侵略性的
10. stereotype [ˈstɛrɪəˌtaɪp] *n.* 刻板印象
11. act upon　遵循⋯行事

Tips for Advanced Readings

Unit 3

Advanced Reading I (page 44)

1. on guard 警戒，提防
2. overworked [`ovə`wɜkt] *adj.* 工作過度的
3. duty [`djutɪ] *n.* 職責；本分，責任
4. as...as possible 盡可能…
5. protector [prə`tɛktə] *n.* 保護者
6. barrier [`bærɪə] *n.* 關卡；障礙
7. interrupt [ˌɪntə`rʌpt] *v.* 使中斷
8. voice mail 語音信箱
9. contact [`kɑntækt] *v.* 聯繫；接觸
10. directly [də`rɛktlɪ] *adv.* 直接地
    direct [də`rɛkt] *adj.* 直接的
11. unless [ʌn`lɛs] *conj.* 除非

Advanced Reading II (page 45)

1. monochronic [ˌmɑnə`krɑnɪk] *adj.* 一次做一件事的
2. polychronic [ˌpɑlɪ`krɑnɪk] *adj.* 一次做多件事的
3. obligation [ˌɑblə`geʃən] *n.* 義務，責任
4. gathering [`gæðrɪŋ] *n.* 聚會，集會
5. engagement [ɪn`gedʒmənt] *n.* 約會；訂婚
6. leisurely [`liʒəlɪ] *adj.; adv.* 悠閒的；悠閒地
   leisure [`liʒə] *n.* 空閒時間，悠閒
7. responsibility [rɪˌspɑnsə`bɪlətɪ] *n.* 責任
   responsible [rɪ`spɑnsəbl] *adj.* 負責的
8. Saudi Arabia 沙烏地阿拉伯
9. hospitality [ˌhɑspɪ`tælətɪ] *n.* (對客人的) 友好款待
   hospitable [`hɑspɪtəbl] *adj.* 好客的
10. therefore [`ðɛrˌfor] *adv.* 因此
11. vary [`vɛrɪ] *v.* 變化，改變
    variety [və`raɪətɪ] *n.* 變化；種類
    various [`vɛrɪəs] *adj.* 各種的

Unit 4

Advanced Reading I (page 56)

1. feedback [`fidˌbæk] *n.* 反應，回應
2. defensive [dɪ`fɛnsɪv] *adj.* 防禦的
   defend [dɪ`fɛnd] *v.* 防禦
3. evaluate [ɪ`væljuˌet] *v.* 評估
4. empathy [`ɛmpəθɪ] *n.* 同感；移情作用
5. persuade [pə`swed] *v.* 說服
6. discuss [dɪ`skʌs] *v.* 討論
   discussion [dɪ`skʌʃən] *n.* 討論
7. in one's shoes 為…設身處地
8. explore [ɪks`plor] *v.* 探索，探測
9. paraphrase [`pærəˌfrez] *v.* 將…釋義
10. universal [ˌjunə`vɜsəl] *adj.* 普世的，普遍的

Advanced Reading II (page 57)

1. professor [prə`fɛsə] *n.* 教授
2. authority [ə`θɔrətɪ] *n.* 權威，威信
3. connection [kə`nɛkʃən] *n.* 關係，關聯
4. Native American 美洲印地安人
5. the elderly 年長者 (總稱)
6. intention [ɪn`tɛnʃən] *n.* 意圖，居心
   intend [ɪn`tɛnd] *v.* 想要，打算

Tips for Advanced Readings

Advanced Reading I (*page 68*)

1. taboo [tə`bu] *n.* 禁忌
2. Nigerian [naɪ`dʒɪrɪən] *n.; adj.* 奈及利亞人 (的)
3. termite [`tɝmaɪt] *n.* 白蟻
4. grasshopper [`græs,hɑpɚ] *n.* 蚱蜢
5. cricket [`krɪkɪt] *n.* 蟋蟀
6. larva [`lɑrvə] *n.* 幼蟲 (複數 larvae)
7. palm weevil　棕櫚象鼻蟲
8. taro [`tɑro] *n.* 芋頭
9. wasp [wɑsp] *n.* 黃蜂
10. Bali [`bɑli] *n.* 峇厘島 (又稱巴厘島，位於印尼)
11. dragonfly [`dræɡən,flaɪ] *n.* 蜻蜓
12. scorpion [`skɔrpɪən] *n.* 蠍子
13. protein [`protiɪn] *n.* 蛋白質
14. poisonous [`pɔɪznəs] *adj.* 有毒的
　　poison [`pɔɪzn] *n.; v.* 毒；使…受毒害

Advanced Reading II (*page 69*)

1. billion [`bɪljən] *n.* 十億
2. Krishna [`krɪʃnə] *n.* 黑天 (印度教神名)
3. cowherd [`kauhɚd] *n.* 牧牛者
4. bull [bul] *n.* 公牛
5. Koran [ko`rɑn] *n.* (the ~) 可蘭經 (回教經典)
6. consist of　由…組成
7. Jain [dʒaɪn] *n.* 耆那教徒
8. cruelty [`kruəltɪ] *n.* 殘酷
　　cruel [kruəl] *adj.* 殘酷的
9. root [rut] *n.* 根

Advanced Reading I (*page 80*)

1. issue [`ɪʃu] *n.* 議題
2. come into play　開始起作用
3. alternation [,ɔltɚ`neʃən] *n.* 交替，相間
4. outspoken [`aut`spokən] *adj.* 直言的
5. Switzerland [`swɪtsɚlənd] *n.* 瑞士
6. quality [`kwɑlətɪ] *n.; adj.* 品質；高級的，優質的

Advanced Reading II (*page 81*)

1. utensil [ju`tɛnsl̩] *n.* (飲食或烹飪的) 器具
2. fuel [`fjuəl] *n.* 燃料
3. chop [tʃɑp] *v.* 剁；砍、劈
4. peasant [`pɛznt] *n.* 農夫；(歐洲的) 雇農
5. metal [`mɛtl̩] *n.* 金屬
6. advantage [əd`væntɪdʒ] *n.* 優勢；好處
7. weapon [`wɛpən] *n.* 武器
8. sensible [`sɛnsəbl̩] *adj.* 明智的；合理的

Tips for Advanced Readings

🎧 **Unit 7**

Advanced Reading I (*page 92*)

1. Holy cow! 天啊！
2. leather [ˈlɛðɚ] *n.* 皮革
3. cowboy [ˈkaʊˌbɔɪ] *n.* (美國西部) 牛仔
4. exclaim [ɪkˈsklem] *v.* 驚呼
5. reciprocate [rɪˈsɪprəˌket] *v.* 回報，報答
6. lily [ˈlɪlɪ] *n.* 百合
7. lotus [ˈlotəs] *n.* 蓮花

Advanced Reading II (*page 93*)

1. unconventional [ˌʌnkənˈvɛnʃənl] *adj.* 異於傳統的，不合常規的
2. aluminum foil 鋁箔紙
3. fabric [ˈfæbrɪk] *n.* 布料
4. recycle [riˈsaɪkl] *v.* 再生利用
5. earring [ˈɪrˌrɪŋ] *n.* 耳環
6. material [məˈtɪrɪəl] *n.* 材料；物質
7. string [strɪŋ] *n.* 粗線；細繩
8. seed [sid] *n.* 種子
9. adopt [əˈdɑpt] *v.* 領養；採用…方式
10. rain forest 雨林
11. solar charger 太陽能充電器

🎧 **Unit 8**

Advanced Reading I (*page 104*)

1. veil [vel] *v.*; *n.* 戴面紗；面紗
2. immigrant [ˈɪməgrənt] *n.* 外來移民
   immigrate [ˈɪməˌgret] *v.* (從他國) 遷居
3. oblige [əˈblaɪdʒ] *v.* 使…有義務…
   obligation [ˌɑbləˈgeʃən] *n.* 義務
4. interfere [ˌɪntɚˈfɪr] *v.* 妨礙；干擾
   interference [ˌɪntɚˈfɪrəns] *n.* 妨礙；干擾
5. Netherlands [ˈnɛðɚləndz] *n.* (the ~) 荷蘭
6. discriminate [dɪˈskrɪməˌnet] *v.* 歧視
   discrimination [dɪˌskrɪməˈneʃən] *n.* 歧視

Advanced Reading II (*page 105*)

1. pinstriped [ˈpɪnˌstraɪpt] *adj.* 細直條紋的 (指布料)
2. crisp [krɪsp] *adj.* 乾淨俐落的；酥脆的
3. sari [ˈsɑri] *n.* 紗麗服 (印度婦女披裹在身上的連身長布)
4. chic [ʃik] *adj.* 時髦的
5. group identity 群體認同
6. overall [ˈovɚˌɔl] *n.* 連身工作服
   overall [ˈovɚˌɔl] *adj.*; *adv.* 整體的；整體上
7. roll up 捲起
8. sleeve [sliv] *n.* 袖子
9. sloppy [ˈslɑpɪ] *adj.* 隨便的；草率的

　　下面有一張圖片及三個相關的問題，請在一分半鐘內完成作答。作答時，請直接回答，不需將題號及題目唸出。

1. How many men and women are there in the picture?
2. What are these people doing?
3. Describe the picture in as much detail as you can.

本聽力測驗部份共有六題。請於聽到播出的英語問句或直述句之後，從以下各題之 A、B、C、D 四個回答或回應中，找出一個最適合的選項作答。每題只播出一遍。

_____ 1. (A) No, thanks.
　　　 (B) Yes, I'm sure.
　　　 (C) Glad to see it, Jeff.
　　　 (D) Hi, Jeff, I am Peter.

_____ 4. (A) Yes, I've met her at a party.
　　　 (B) Yes, Molly has met her.
　　　 (C) Yes, Molly is fine.
　　　 (D) Yes, she is her best friend.

_____ 2. (A) What are these, Sally?
　　　 (B) Hi, Sally, nice to meet you.
　　　 (C) I'm sorry, Sally.
　　　 (D) How was it, Sally?

_____ 5. (A) Yes, Josh hasn't called you.
　　　 (B) No, Josh didn't call me.
　　　 (C) Nice to meet you, Josh.
　　　 (D) Can you call Josh?

_____ 3. (A) My name is Roger Liang.
　　　 (B) I can call you later, Steven.
　　　 (C) Yes, my name is Roger Liang.
　　　 (D) No, I cannot call you Steven.

_____ 6. (A) No, I've met Judy.
　　　 (B) Yes, I haven't met her.
　　　 (C) Judy is not in the office.
　　　 (D) Glad to meet you, Judy.

I *Based on Advanced Reading I, choose the correct answer to each of the following questions.*

_____ 1. It is important to learn how to communicate with people from other cultures, _____ using proper forms of address.
(A) to be included
(B) included
(C) including
(D) is including

_____ 2. _____ with the Americans, the Japanese are very strict about using proper forms of address.
(A) To compare
(B) Compared
(C) Comparing
(D) Be compared

_____ 3. To the Japanese, there is a clear _____ between a business relationship and a personal relationship.
(A) impression
(B) custom
(C) difference
(D) value

_____ 4. To the Americans, formal forms of address are _____ for greeting someone for the first time.
(A) common
(B) eager
(C) strict
(D) strange

II *Fill in each of the blanks with one of the words below based on Advanced Reading I. Change the word form if necessary.*

proper	*title*	*valuable*	*observe*
compare	*impression*	*expert*	

1. Creating good first _____ is important in building business relationships.

2. _____ have been hired to teach company employees how to communicate with people from other cultures.

3. When your travel to a foreign country, always _____ the local etiquette for addressing others.

4. In the U.S., "Ms." is a _____ for every woman—whether she is married or not.

5. When a businessperson _____ the business culture in Japan with that in the U.S., he or she will see the differences between the two.

6. The understanding of cultural differences is _____ to those who work in international business.

7. Learning _____ forms of address is an important part of business communication.

I *Choose the correct answers based on Advanced Reading II.*

(   ) 1. In American and _____ cultures, an arm's length is the proper distance between two people during a conversation.

(A) Arabic   (B) Latin   (C) European   (D) Asian

(   ) 2. Which of the following statements is true?

(A) People in Italy and Spain usually arrive for meetings later than the scheduled time.

(B) In Asia, businesspeople pay little attention to personal matters.

(C) Most Latin Americans prefer a long personal distance during a conversation.

(D) In the U.S., don't expect your business partners to arrive for meetings on time.

(   ) 3. _____ prefer to start business relationships on a personal level.

(A) The Americans   (B) The Europeans

(C) The Latin Americans   (D) The Asians

II *Choose the correct answer to each of the following questions based on Advanced Reading II.*

(   ) 1. In the U.S., being late for over 15 minutes is considered _____.

(A) wise   (B) valuable   (C) usual   (D) rude

(   ) 2. It is always a _____ to work with people from other cultures.

(A) change   (B) challenge   (C) distance   (D) difference

III *Match the items on the left with those on the right based on Advanced Reading II.*

1. In the U.S., ...

2. To the Asians...

3. In Latin America, ...

4. To the Italians, ...

...it is not unusual to be a bit late for meetings.

...be sure to arrive 5 or 10 minutes early for meetings.

...it is common to start business relationships on a personal level.

...people like to be close to each other during conversations.

下面有一張圖片及三個相關的問題，請在一分半鐘內完成作答。作答時，請直接回答，不需將題號及題目唸出。

1. What is the man holding in his hands?

2. What is the woman doing for the man?

3. Describe the picture in as much detail as you can.

本聽力測驗部份共有六題。請於聽到播出的一段英語對話之後，從以下各題之 A、B、C、D 四個選項中，找出一個最適合的作答。每題只播出一遍。

1. (A) Mr. Oaks answers the phone.
   (B) The caller is Karen Miles.
   (C) Mr. Oaks takes a message from Ms. Miles.
   (D) Mr. Oaks will not be in today.

4. (A) Judy's mother takes a message from David.
   (B) Judy will call David later.
   (C) Judy's mother answers the phone.
   (D) Judy's mother calls and asks for David.

 2. (A) Stanley calls and asks for Amanda.
   (B) Stanley calls and asks for Troy.
   (C) Amanda calls and asks for Troy.
   (D) Troy calls and asks for Stanley.

 5. (A) Ms. Kennedy will call back later today.
   (B) Ms. Kenney wants Mr. Chen to call her back tomorrow.
   (C) Mr. Chen asks Ms. Kennedy to call back tomorrow.
   (D) Mr. Chen is coming in tomorrow.

 3. (A) Mr. Davis asks if Ms. Larson has received his e-mail.
   (B) Mr. Larson asks if Ms. Davis is in the office.
   (C) Ms. Larson calls Mr. Davis.
   (D) Ms. Davis answers the phone.

 6. (A) Aaron calls and asks for Vicky.
   (B) Aaron will call back in one and a half hours.
   (C) Vicky takes a message from Aaron.
   (D) Vicky tells Aaron to call back in one and a half hours.

I   *Based on Advanced Reading I, mark each of the following statements with T (True) or F (False).*

_____ 1. Men usually focus on "sharing" and "feelings" when it comes to communication styles.

_____ 2. Women sometimes complain that men are insensitive.

_____ 3. To communicate better with women, be sure to ask for and share thoughts, feelings, and opinions.

_____ 4. It is important for men to build a sense of agreement.

_____ 5. In the process of making decisions, women like to make sure everyone is involved.

II   *Choose the correct answers based on Advanced Reading I.*

_____ 1. In the workplace, women tend to spend most of their time _____ a sense of "agreement."
(A) to create
(B) to be creating
(C) getting created
(D) creating

_____ 2. Before making decisions as a group, women usually want to make sure _____ everyone is involved.
(A) which
(B) in which
(C) that
(D) in that

_____ 3. According to traditional gender stereotypes, men like to focus _____ information when it comes to communication.
(A) on
(B) in
(C) from
(D) of

_____ 4. Differences in communication styles can _____ misunderstandings between the two genders.
(A) make
(B) do
(C) take
(D) cause

I　*Based on Advanced Reading II, mark each of the following statements with T (True) or F (False).*

_____ 1. About 16 percent of corporate executives in America's top companies are women.

_____ 2. The American society is now able to treat men and woman equally in the workplace because of the Equal Rights Amendment.

_____ 3. Traditionally, men are believed to be aggressive and strong.

_____ 4. What a person can do at work is not determined by his or her gender.

_____ 5. Gender stereotypes claim that it is better for women to hold positions of support.

II　*Choose the correct answers based on Advanced Reading II.*

_____ 1. Women _____ only 2 percent of chief executive officers in America's top companies.
(A) bring up
(B) add up
(C) make up
(D) give up

_____ 2. One of the reasons _____ including the Equal Rights Amendment in the American Constitution is to ensure equality between men and women.
(A) to
(B) for
(C) in
(D) of

_____ 3. Up to 2007, the Equal Rights Amendment has been in place _____ 85 years.
(A) in
(B) ×
(C) for
(D) with

_____ 4. There could be a number of _____ for the inequalities between men and women in the U.S. today, such as traditional beliefs and gender stereotypes.
(A) result
(B) results
(C) causes
(D) cause

　　下面有兩張圖片及三個相關的問題，請在一分半鐘內完成作答。作答時，請直接回答，不需將題號及題目唸出。

1. What are the man and the woman doing?
2. Where are the man and the woman?
3. Describe the pictures in as much detail as you can.

🎧 本聽力測驗部份共有六題。請於聽到播出的一段英語對話之後，從以下各題之 A、B、C、D 四個選項中，找出一個最適合的作答。每題只播出一遍。

1. (A) The man wants to buy the pink shirt.
(B) The woman wants to buy the white shirt.
(C) The man will try on the pink shirt.
(D) The woman will try on the white shirt.

2. (A) The woman is on her way out.
(B) The woman doesn't like the taste of coffee.
(C) The man will stay home.
(D) The man wants to have some ice cream.

3. (A) The man prefers to take a taxi.
(B) The woman agrees to take the bus.
(C) The man and the woman are at the airport.
(D) The man and the woman are at the hotel.

4. (A) The woman wants to share the pizza.
(B) The woman prefers to have something greasy.
(C) The man is on a diet.
(D) The woman had salad for lunch.

5. (A) The woman doesn't like the food in Japan.
(B) The man prefers Bangkok to Tokyo.
(C) The man and the woman are going to Bangkok.
(D) The man and woman like the food in Thailand.

6. (A) The man will stay home.
(B) The man is on his way out to the beach.
(C) The woman is putting on some sunblock.
(D) The woman would rather go to the beach.

I

Based on Advanced Reading I, match the items on the left with those on the right.

...see themselves as their bosses' protectors.

1. In America, secretaries...

...try to be as helpful as possible.

...do their best to make visitors feel welcome.

2. In France, secretaries...

...remind their bosses of other appointments when they're still in a meeting.

II

Choose the correct answers for each of the blanks based on Advanced Reading I.

_____1_____ what most of us think, secretaries are not always women. Even if the secretary is a woman, what she has to do is much more than just "sit there and be beautiful." In fact, working as a secretary involves various _____2_____ that require lots of time, patience, and energy. _____3_____, most secretaries have to do paper work for their bosses. That _____4_____ typing reports, copying papers, and so on. Also, they have to deal with all kinds of people who want to meet with their bosses: customers, employees, etc. That's not all. Sometimes, secretaries have to go on business trips with their bosses.

Who says it's easy to work as a secretary?

_____ 1. (A) As	(B) Adding to	(C) Compared with	(D) Unlike
_____ 2. (A) a duty	(B) duties	(C) work	(D) works
_____ 3. (A) In addition	(B) In fact	(C) For example	(D) As a result
_____ 4. (A) includes	(B) takes	(C) has	(D) needs

I

Based on Advanced Reading II, match the items on the left with those on the right.

...are mostly in Asia, the U.S., and some parts of Europe.

...are mostly in the Arab World and Latin America.

1. Monochronic cultures...

...view "time" with flexibility.

2. Polychronic cultures...

...place a great deal of importance on "time."

II

Choose the correct answers based on Advanced Reading II.

(　　　) 1. In Mexico, a *siesta* _____.

(A) lasts for less than an hour

(B) is an afternoon break

(C) is an important holiday

(D) is a special type of appointment

(　　　) 2. Which of the following statements is true?

(A) Punctuality is more important than hospitality in Saudi Arabia.

(B) It is OK to cancel or be late for social gathering in Korea.

(C) To the Mexicans, family responsibilities come before business obligations.

(D) It is never acceptable to be late for a social engagement in the U.S.

(　　　) 3. In Saudi Arabia, _____.

(A) appointments are scheduled for specific times of the day

(B) a great deal of importance is placed on time

(C) flexibility of time does not apply to religious prayers

(D) plans are always kept unchanged

下面有一張圖片及三個相關的問題，請在一分半鐘內完成作答。作答時，請直接回答，不需將題號及題目唸出。

1. Why do you think the woman looks uncomfortable?
2. Where do you think they are?
3. Describe the picture in as much detail as you can.

本聽力測驗部份共有六題。請於聽到播出的一段英語對話之後，從以下各題之 A、B、C、D 四個選項中，找出一個最適合的作答。每題只播出一遍。

1. (A) The man wants to lose weight.
   (B) The woman asks the man to lose some weight.
   (C) The man asks the woman how much she weighs.
   (D) The woman asks the man how she can lose weight.

2. (A) The woman asks the man about his old job.
   (B) The woman asks the man how much the company is going to pay him.
   (C) It took the man a long time to make the decision.
   (D) It took the man a long time to answer the question.

3. (A) The woman wants to know who the CEO of her company is.
   (B) The woman asks the man how old he is.
   (C) The man wants to know the woman's age.
   (D) The man asks the woman if she is the CEO of a huge company.

4. (A) The man asks the woman about her children.
   (B) The woman asks the man about his age.
   (C) The man has seen the woman in the gym before.
   (D) The woman has two children.

5. (A) The man didn't go to work yesterday.
   (B) The woman asked the man about his job.
   (C) The man asked the woman about her health.
   (D) The woman went to the hospital yesterday.

6. (A) The man asks if the woman works at a bank.
   (B) The man asks the woman to give him NT$30,000 every month.
   (C) The woman has enough money to buy an apartment of her own.
   (D) The woman pays NT$30,000 for her apartment every month.

I *Based on Advanced Reading I, mark each of the following statements with T (True) or F (False).*

_____ 1. A good listener should give positive feedback and encourage the speaker to talk.

_____ 2. To show empathy, listeners should learn to paraphrase the words of the speakers.

_____ 3. Nodding to speakers is a defensive behavior.

_____ 4. Both the speaker and the listener should ask each other appropriate questions that indicate interest.

_____ 5. To evaluate a speaker's message, a good listener must learn to express disagreement before the speaker finishes his or her words.

II *Choose the correct answers based on Advanced Reading I.*

_____ 1. Studies have shown that _____ estimated 6912 languages are spoken in the world today.
(A) ×
(B) an
(C) about
(D) almost

_____ 3. Showing empathy involves _____ speakers' emotions.
(A) in exploring
(B) exploring of
(C) exploring
(D) to explore

_____ 2. Listeners should keep themselves _____ questions that indicate judgment.
(A) to ask
(B) in asking
(C) asking
(D) from asking

_____ 4. It is important for listeners to _____ speakers to finish what they have to say.
(A) let
(B) allow
(C) make
(D) wait

I *Choose the correct answers based on Advanced Reading II.*

(　　) 1. To the Native Americans, lasting eye contact _____.

　　　　(A) makes it easier to bring people together

　　　　(B) helps create a sense of connection

　　　　(C) makes it possible to steal a person's soul

　　　　(D) is a way of showing respect

(　　) 2. The Japanese tend to _____ during conversations.

　　　　(A) give lasting eye contact

　　　　(B) avoid eye contact to hide secrets

　　　　(C) make frequent eye contact with speakers

　　　　(D) look at speakers' necks instead of their eyes

(　　) 3. What eye contact means to a person depends on _____.

　　　　(A) what language the person speaks

　　　　(B) where the person is from

　　　　(C) how old the person is

　　　　(D) what the person does for a living

(　　) 4. In many Asian cultures, it is rude to make direct eye contact with _____ or

　　　　_____.

　　　　(A) those in higher positions; women

　　　　(B) Westerners; the elderly

　　　　(C) Westerners; women

　　　　(D) those in higher positions; the elderly

(　　) 5. In _____ and _____ cultures, avoiding eye contact is a sign of

　　　　dishonesty.

　　　　(A) Japanese; American　　　　　　　(B) Japanese; Native American

　　　　(C) European; American　　　　　　　(D) European; Native American

II *Based on Advanced Reading II, answer each of the following questions with at least one complete sentence.*

1. What does frequent lasting eye contact mean to the Japanese?

　_____

　_____

2. According to the first paragraph, why is the professor becoming annoyed?

　_____

　_____

　　下面有一張圖片及四個相關的問題，請在一分半鐘內完成作答。作答時，請直接回答，不需將題號及題目唸出。

1. Where are the man and the woman?

2. What is on the table?

3. Why are the man and the woman eating in this place?

4. Describe the picture in as much detail as you can.

🎧40 本聽力測驗部份共有六題，情境皆為餐廳中所發生的對話。請於聽到播出的英語問句或直述句之後，從以下各題之 A、B、C、D 四個回答或回應中，找出一個最適合的選項作答。每題只播出一遍。

1. (A) No, we'd like to have some fries.
   (B) I'd like to have some fried chicken.
   (C) Yes. Please bring us some water.
   (D) The steak is delicious.

2. (A) Yes. I think we're fine here.
   (B) No. You are too late for the show.
   (C) Yes. Please ship the order tomorrow.
   (D) No. We are not ready yet.

3. (A) Yes. Everyone is here now.
   (B) No. The food is already cold.
   (C) Yes. Please take the empty plates away.
   (D) No. A few more minutes are not what I want.

4. (A) No. I didn't order the ice cream.
   (B) No. I am not ready to order.
   (C) Yes. The steak is too raw.
   (D) Yes. I'd like to have some more water.

5. (A) I like it very much.
   (B) I don't like steaks.
   (C) I'd like to have it well-done.
   (D) I would like to have it later.

6. (A) Let me get you the drinks first.
   (B) I'm terribly sorry about that.
   (C) Here is your extra syrup.
   (D) I'm sure it's on the order.

I Based on Advanced Reading I, mark each of the following statements with T (True) or F (False).

_____ 1. To the Japanese, palm weevils and scorpions can be made into delicacies.

_____ 2. In Bali, roasted termites are part of the local diet.

_____ 3. The taboo on eating insects has nothing to do with science.

_____ 4. Both the Nigerians and the Japanese eat grasshoppers.

_____ 5. People have not learned how to deal with poisonous insects without getting poisoned.

II Fill in each of the blanks with one of the words below based on Advanced Reading I. Change the word form if necessary.

fry	roasted	boiling	basic	barbecue
taboo	take	full	source	dealing

1. In Nigeria, termites are _____ over a fire before they are served as food.

2. Some insects are regarded as excellent _____ of protein.

3. The fear that eating insects is bad for our health has no scientific _____.

4. The Balinese _____ or boil dragonflies with ginger, garlic, and coconut milk.

5. Eating insects is a _____ that is beyond most Westeners' imagination.

6. The Nigerians, after _____ out the insides of crickets, turn them into a delicacy.

7. Today, when people _____ with poisonous insects, they've learned how to cook them without getting poisoned.

8. Insects, when they are _____ cooked, are safe to eat most of the time.

9. In Japan, wasp larvae are _____ before they are served on the table.

10. In northern Thailand, people turn scorpions into snacks by _____ them.

I   *Choose the correct answers based on Advanced Reading II.*

(   ) 1. The traditional Jain diet does not include _____ .
     (A) eggs   (B) fish   (C) cheese   (D) all of the above

(   ) 2. Which of the following statements is NOT true?
     (A) Jains believe in peace and love for all living things.
     (B) Jains expect themselves to do what Krishna did, loving and protecting cattle.
     (C) Hindu Indians consider it a taboo to eat hamburgers or anything made of beef.
     (D) Muslim Indians believe that those who eat pork will become unclean also.

(   ) 3. To some _____ , it is a taboo to eat root vegetables.
     (A) Jain Indians   (B) Hindu Indians   (C) Muslim Indians   (D) American Indians

(   ) 4. According to the Koran, _____ are unclean animals.
     (A) pigs   (B) cattle   (C) dogs   (D) all animals

(   ) 5. Which of the following statements is true?
     (A) Hindus consider beef unclean because the Koran teaches them so.
     (B) Muslims refuse to eat anything that involves cruelty to animals.
     (C) In India, dietary taboos vary from one religious group to another.
     (D) All Jain Indians believe that taking away the root of a plant is a form of cruelty.

II   *Based on Advanced Reading II, answer each of the following questions with at least one complete sentence.*

1. How are cattle, especially cows, treated by Hindu Indians?

_____

_____

2. What do Muslims believe about "eating pork"?

_____

_____

　　下面有兩張圖片及四個相關的問題，請在一分半鐘內完成作答。作答時，請直接回答，不需將題號及題目唸出。

1. How would you describe the man's hair?

2. In terms of skin tone, how would you describe the woman?

3. How is the woman's physical figure in comparison with the man's?

4. Describe the pictures in as much detail as you can.

🎧(48) 本聽力測驗部份共有六題。請於聽到播出的一段英語對話之後，從以下各題之 A、B、C、D 四個選項中，找出一個最適合的作答。每題只播出一遍。

1. (A) The woman is heading to a restaurant.
   (B) The woman asks if Jessica wants to go shopping with her.
   (C) The man is going to the mall with the woman.
   (D) The man is going out with Jessica for lunch.

2. (A) The woman can't go out with the man on Saturday.
   (B) The man asks the woman to have lunch with him on Saturday.
   (C) The woman asks the man to call her tomorrow.
   (D) The man won't go out with the woman tomorrow.

3. (A) The man's birthday is in May.
   (B) The woman's schedule is full next Wednesday.
   (C) The woman is going to the man's birthday party.
   (D) The man is planning for the woman's birthday party.

4. (A) The woman moves the dinner appointment to another day.
   (B) The man has a dinner appointment on Friday.
   (C) The woman will have dinner with the man on Friday.
   (D) The man is asking the woman to go out with him.

5. (A) The woman and her sister are going to Tokyo next month.
   (B) The man and the woman's sister are going to Tokyo next week.
   (C) The woman has no interest in going to Tokyo next week.
   (D) The man and the woman are going to Tokyo next month.

6. (A) The man and the woman are going to finish the paper together.
   (B) The man and the woman are going for a swim.
   (C) The man is going home at one thirty.
   (D) The woman is going home at two o'clock.

I *Based on Advanced Reading I, check (✓) the ideas that are included in the reading.*

☐ 1. In France, the custom of arranging seats in the "man-woman-man-woman" alternation dates back to the Middle Ages.

☐ 2. Few issues come into play when it comes to international dining.

☐ 3. North Americans are not strict about seating arrangements.

☐ 4. The French usually avoid talking about religion at the dinner table.

☐ 5. In certain parts of the Middle East, men and women eat only in separate rooms, but not in different locations.

☐ 6. Some Americans do not ask for opinions when they talk about politics.

☐ 7. Gift-giving has nothing to do with dining etiquette, especially during international meals.

II *Choose the correct answers based on Advanced Reading I.*

(   ) 1. If you are invited _____ a dinner party, be sure to learn the dining etiquette in the host's or hostess's culture.
    (A) in   (B) to   (C) at   (D) toward

(   ) 2. _____ the culture, certain objects should never be presented as gifts at the dinner table.
    (A) In addition to   (B) As for   (C) By means of   (D) Depending on

(   ) 3. In France, people usually don't talk about jobs. That's why they won't ask you what you do _____.
    (A) for a life   (B) to live   (C) for a living   (D) to make a life

(   ) 4. In some Middle Eastern countries, _____ men and women eat in separate rooms, don't expect to sit next to your boyfriend or girlfriend when you go to a dinner party.
    (A) which   (B) how   (C) ✕   (D) where

I *Based on Advanced Reading II, mark each of the following statements with T (True) or F (False).*

_____ 1. The Asians' preference for chopsticks results from some cultural beliefs that are common in Asian cultures.

_____ 2. Fuel and meat were rare in ancient Europe.

_____ 3. In ancient times, the Europeans chopped food into bite-size pieces so that everyone could have a piece.

_____ 4. It is inappropriate for an Indian to use his or her left hand to pick up food.

_____ 5. In the Middle East, a person's right hand should be kept clean at all times.

II *Based on Advanced Reading II, match the following items with those in the box.*

1. In ancient Asia, _____.　　　2. In ancient Europe, _____.

(A) chopping food into bite-size pieces made it easier to save fuel
(B) meat was usually cooked in large pieces
(C) meat was rarely available to peasants
(D) diners brought with them sharp utensils to cut meat
(E) forks and knives gave diners the advantage of having sharp weapons in case the meal turned into a bloody fight

III *Based on Advanced Reading II, answer each of the following questions with at least one complete sentence.*

1. What is the left hand usually used for in India and the Middle East?

_____

_____

2. What do the Middle Easterners believe about "tasting the food"?

_____

_____

下面有兩張圖片及四個相關的問題，請在一分半鐘內完成作答。作答時，請直接回答，不需將題號及題目唸出。

Picture 1

Picture 2

1. In Picture 1, what does the man do?

2. In Picture 1, what is the man doing for the woman?

3. In Picture 2, what is the woman doing?

4. Describe the pictures in as much detail as you can.

🎧 本聽力測驗部份共有六題。請於聽到播出的英語對話之後，從以下各題之 A、B、C、D 四個選項中，找出一個最適合的作答。每題只播出一遍。

_____ 1. (A) The woman doesn't have the receipt with her.
(B) The man will give the woman a new dress for free.
(C) The woman insists on getting a refund.
(D) The man asks if the woman would like to buy a new dress.

_____ 2. (A) The woman agrees to fix the man's DVD player.
(B) The man doesn't have the warranty with him.
(C) The woman can't exchange the DVD player for the man.
(D) The man asks the woman for the receipt.

_____ 3. (A) The man agrees to refund the digital camera without the warranty.
(B) The woman wants to get a refund on the digital camera.
(C) The man agrees to give the woman another warranty.
(D) The woman has the warranty, but not the receipt.

_____ 4. (A) The man doesn't have the warranty with him.
(B) The woman agrees to refund the cellphone.
(C) The man knows how to fix the cellphone.
(D) The woman asks the man to leave the cellphone there.

_____ 5. (A) The man agrees to give the woman a NT$2,000 discount.
(B) The woman asks the man to let her exchange the PDA.
(C) The man has to pay NT$2,000 more for the new PDA.
(D) The woman will get a NT$2,000 refund on the PDA.

_____ 6. (A) The man will get a refund on the CD within a month.
(B) The woman agrees to let the man exchange the CD.
(C) The man bought the CD a month ago.
(D) The woman asks the man to come back within a week.

I

Choose the correct answers based on Advanced Reading I.

(　　) 1. David bought a leather jacket for Kumar, and he was very proud _____ the gift.
　　　　(A) in　　　　　(B) on　　　　　(C) for　　　　　(D) of

(　　) 2. The Indians usually _____ what they receive. In other words, if they receive something expensive from a guest, they will offer an expensive gift to the guest also.
　　　　(A) regard　　　(B) reciprocate　　(C) repeat　　　(D) refund

(　　) 3. Lilies or lotus blossoms _____ unlucky in Japan.
　　　　(A) consider　　　　　　　　　(B) are to consider
　　　　(C) are considered　　　　　　(D) considered to be

(　　) 4. In India, expensive gifts or anything made of leather _____ likely to offend the recipient.
　　　　(A) is　　　　　(B) are　　　　　(C) do　　　　　(D) will

II

Choose the correct answers.

(　　) 1. In Japan, avoid giving gifts that consist of the number "_____" and "_____."
　　　　(A) four; nine　　(B) six; nine　　(C) four; six　　(D) two; six

(　　) 2. When offering gifts to the Indians, _____.
　　　　(A) buy something expensive at all times
　　　　(B) open the gifts right away
　　　　(C) choose something made of leather
　　　　(D) wrap the gifts in bright colors

(　　) 3. Which of the following statements is true?
　　　　(A) Gift giving has nothing to do with how it is presented to the recipient.
　　　　(B) Red, yellow, and green are all unlucky colors in India .
　　　　(C) When giving gifts to the Japanese, use both hands in a polite manner.
　　　　(D) Gifts of white flowers, such as lilies or lotus blossoms, are always appreciated in Japanese homes.

(　　) 4. According to the story in the first paragraph, Kumar felt offended because _____.
　　　　(A) a leather jacket is too expensive of a gift for him
　　　　(B) David offered the gift with his left hand
　　　　(C) the cow is sacred to Hindus
　　　　(D) David opened the gift in front of him

I

Check (✓) the ideas that are included in Advanced Reading II.

☐ 1. We can all learn to give presents and at the same time, help protect the environment.

☐ 2. Most of the paper we use to wrap gifts is recycled.

☐ 3. If you use strings, wool, or ribbons to tie up the present, then the wrapping paper can be used again.

☐ 4. Zoo animals are too expensive to adopt.

☐ 5. Quality alcohol and sweets make the best gifts that produce no waste.

☐ 6. A solar charger for iPods is a gift that helps save energy.

☐ 7. Wrapping gifts in plastic bags is good for the planet.

II

Choose the correct answers based on Advanced Reading II.

_____ 1. If you _____ a donation to an environmental charity, you are actually supporting projects that help save rain forests or endangered species.
(A) make
(B) do
(C) send
(D) reciprocate

_____ 2. Why not think _____ something you are good at and turn it into a gift?
(A) for
(B) through
(C) of
(D) ✕

_____ 3. If you make a gift _____ your time or help, there won't be anything to throw away afterwards.
(A) in
(B) of
(C) by
(D) for

_____ 4. Plants, seeds, or a bird house _____ a great gift for those who love the outdoors.
(A) make
(B) offer
(C) makes
(D) offers

　　下面有三張圖片及四個相關的問題，請在一分半鐘內完成作答。作答時，請直接針對圖片中人物的個性回答，不需將題號及題目唸出。

Picture 1

Picture 2

Picture 3

1. The man in Picture 1 has been waiting for his girlfriend for only two minutes. How would you describe his personality?

2. Suppose the woman in Picture 2 is your boss, and she is telling you, "Do everything you can to close the deal," how would you describe her personality?

3. If the man in Picture 3 falls asleep all the time at work, how would you describe his personality?

4. Describe the pictures in as much detail as you can.

本聽力測驗部份共有六題。請於聽到播出的英語對話之後，從以下各題之 A、B、C、D 四個選項中，找出一個最適合的作答。每題只播出一遍。

1. (A) Sandy is more easygoing than Julie.
   (B) The man went out on a date last week.
   (C) Sandy is smarter than Julie.
   (D) The man went out with Julie.

4. (A) The man will vote for Mr. McCain.
   (B) The woman prefers someone intelligent.
   (C) Mr. McCain is a man of determination.
   (D) Mr. Dean is very aggressive.

2. (A) Danny is the new marketing director.
   (B) The man prefers to hire Danny.
   (C) The woman prefers someone creative.
   (D) Ben is creative.

5. (A) The man thinks Rachael is uptight.
   (B) Ruby gets along with the children better.
   (C) The man agrees to have Ruby babysit the children.
   (D) All Ruby does is play computer games with the children.

3. (A) Ms. Wang is not a teacher.
   (B) Ms. Yang has no patience with students.
   (C) Ms. Wang is hard-working.
   (D) Ms. Yang doesn't know how to teach.

6. (A) Dr. Baldwin is always late for classes.
   (B) Dr. Liang has a great sense of humor.
   (C) Dr. Baldwin is a man.
   (D) Dr. Liang is good at teaching.

I *Based on Advanced Reading I, mark each of the following statements with T (True) or F (False).*

_____ 1. Samira Haddad is a Muslim woman who reported her case of discrimination in the Netherlands.

_____ 2. A burka covers half of a Muslim woman's face.

_____ 3. The woman in Britain was fired from her job because she refused to wear a burka.

_____ 4. Samira Haddad did not wear a burka when she was interviewed for a position at the Islamic College in Amsterdam.

_____ 5. Learning about cultural differences is no different from accepting them.

II *Fill in each of the blanks with one of the words below based on Advanced Reading I. Change the word form if necessary.*

interference	discriminate	oblige
observance	employ	religion

1. Wearing a burka is one of the _____ rules for Muslim women.

2. Some have voiced their concern that in the workplace, wearing a burka is likely to _____ with job performance.

3. Every government has a(n) _____ to ensure equality for its people.

4. After moving to a new country, some immigrants continue to _____ traditional customs in their culture while others choose to "do as the Romans do."

5. To those immigrants who can't speak English, finding _____ in the U.S. can be very difficult, sometimes impossible.

6. After the 911 Attack, it has been reported that Muslims in the U.S. have experienced _____ in the job market.

I

Choose the correct answers based on Advanced Reading II.

_____ 1. In Europe, dressing in _____ is very chic, but the color is associated with death in some countries.
(A) blue
(B) white
(C) black
(D) brown

_____ 2. Which of the following statements is true?
(A) Clothing is influenced by few local factors.
(B) The universal dress code for all business cultures does not exist.
(C) Differences in clothing are common when group identity is highly valued.
(D) Saris are usually made in white.

_____ 3. In the story, _____ wears a Giorgio Armani suit.
(A) the American
(B) the German
(C) the Englishman
(D) the Italian

_____ 4. In _____, saris are usually made in bright colors.
(A) France
(B) Germany
(C) English
(D) India

II

Based on Advanced Reading II, answer each of the following questions with at least one complete sentence.

1. What influences clothing preferences and choices in cultures around the world?

_____

_____

2. In terms of clothing, what might a Japanese manager wear when he or she visits a production site?

_____

_____

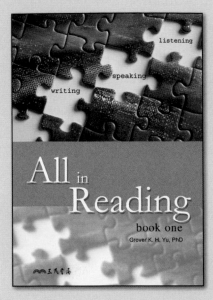

ALL IN READING book one

全方位英文閱讀   余光雄 編著

本書題材以「文化比較」為主軸,將內容延伸至聽、說、讀、寫四大層面上:

1. 本書以增進學生英文閱讀和理解能力為目標。課文選自國外教材,主題生活化,讀來活潑有趣。
2. 每課均有聽、說、讀、寫四大單元,讓學生均衡發展英文四大能力。
3. 版面設計採用豐富多元的照片和插圖,教學使用更活潑;標題依照四大能力分類設計,功能分類一目了然。
4. 本書並附有教師手冊、朗讀光碟及電子教學投影片。

HOSPITALITY ENGLISH AND CONVERSATION

餐旅英文與會話 I

黃招憲、David Walter Goodman 編著

1. 本書目標為培養學生簡單英文會話能力,因應其工作基本需求。
2. 共分12課,每課針對會話主題及溝通功能(functions)所設計,包括 Getting Started (暖身活動)、Conversations (對話)、Useful Expressions (實用語)、Oral Practice (口語練習) 和 Listening Practice (聽力練習) 等單元,幫助學生建立穩固的會話基礎。
3. 附有教師手冊及由專業外籍人士所錄製的朗讀光碟,以讓學生熟悉 native speaker 的發音和語調。

ENJOY READING 悅讀50　　　　　　　　　王隆興 編著

1. 精選50篇多元主題的文章，篇篇妙筆生花，精彩好讀。
2. 命題方向符合各類大考趨勢，讓您熟能生巧，輕取高分。
3. 特聘優質外籍作者親撰文章，語法用字純正道地。
4. 文章程度符合大考中心公佈之單字表中4000字的範圍，難度適中。
5. 本書備有解析本。

英語口語練習 I~VI　　　　　　　　蔡玟玲、吳企方 編著

1. 本書融合聽、說、讀、寫四個部份，以溝通式教學 (communicative approach)為導向。
2. 就功能而言，每課分成兩個階段：第一階段包括閱讀、重要單字等的練習活動；第二階段主要功能為增進聽力或口語表達能力，如代換練習、角色扮演等。
3. 全書編寫以日常生活英語會話為主軸，除適合課堂教學外，亦適合自修。
4. 本書備有教師手冊。

英文寫作練習 I~IV　　　　　　　　　　　黃素月 編著

本套書適合學習英文多年，但仍欠缺完整寫作訓練的讀者。在教學設計上，本書運用多種教學理論，作者群教學經驗豐富，妥善巧妙地將理論與實際教學經驗連結，是國內少見的本土版完整英文寫作教材。

本套書並附有豐富的範文及例句。書中所選範文，皆與青少年生活、重要時事以及其他國家的有趣文化和社會現象息息相關。寫作活動的安排由淺入深，每個活動皆標示難易度，可配合讀者的程度。本套書並備有教師手冊及解答本。

實用英文文法　　　馬洵、劉紅英、郭立穎 編著，龔慧懿 編審

1. 文字說明深入淺出、讓您輕鬆學習。
2. 用字簡明精確、易懂易記，絕不讓您讀得「霧煞煞」。
3. 以圖表方式歸納、條列文法重點，讓您對文法規則一目了然。
4. 書中文法搭配上千條例句，情境兼具普遍性和專業性，並附有中文翻譯，便於自學。

國家圖書館出版品預行編目資料

HEAD START I／車蓓群 (Patricia Che)主編.－－
初版一刷.－－臺北市：三民，2007
　　冊；　公分

ISBN 978－957－14－4824－4　（第一冊：平裝）

1. 英語 2. 讀本

805.18　　　　　　　　　　　　　　96014959

© 　HEAD　　START　　I

主　　編	車蓓群 (Patricia Che)
責任編輯	廖健華　許嘉諾
版面設計	蔡季吟
插畫設計	王孟婷　朱正明　吳　騏　許珮淨

發 行 人	劉振強
著作財產權人	三民書局股份有限公司
發 行 所	三民書局股份有限公司
	地址　臺北市復興北路386號
	電話　(02)25006600
	郵撥帳號　0009998－5
門 市 部	(復北店) 臺北市復興北路386號
	(重南店) 臺北市重慶南路一段61號

出版日期	初版一刷　2007年9月
編　　號	S 807100

行政院新聞局登記證局版臺業字第○二○○號

有著作權‧不准侵害

ISBN　978－957－14－4824－4　（第一冊：平裝）

http://www.sanmin.com.tw　三民網路書店

※本書如有缺頁、破損或裝訂錯誤，請寄回本公司更換。